# CADENCE AND COUNTERPOINT
## Documenting Santal Musical Traditions



Edited by Johannes Beltz
Marie-Eve Celio-Scheurer
Ruchira Ghose

NIYOGI
BOOKS

This publication is dedicated to Babudhan Murmu, Bhulu Murmu, Shibdhan Murmu, Sonadhan Murmu, Sangita Murmu, Jashodi Murmu and the extended Santal community.

CONTENTS

APPENDIX

# PHOTOGRAPHS FROM THE 1950s



Alain Daniélou
Raymond Burnier

Photographs taken by Alain Daniélou (1907–1994) and Raymond Burnier (1912–1968) in the 1950s at a Santal village close to Santiniketan. They are from the Daniélou photographic archives (more than 8000 slides taken from 1935 to 1955) kept at the India Europe Foundation for New Dialogues (FIND) in Zagarolo, Rome. FIND was set up by Alain Daniélou. Its President is Jacques Cloarec.

Alain Daniélou was a French musicologist, Sanskrit scholar and Indologist, who spent a large part of his life in India (1932–1958). He was accompanied on his travels by the Swiss photographer Raymond Burnier. They were among the first to photograph India's ancient temple complexes and their works on the temples of Khajuraho were exhibited at New York's Metropolitan Museum. Daniélou travelled with Burnier to Bhubaneswar, Konarak, and many other historic sites in Central India and Rajasthan. The photographs of these journeys are archived at FIND, and also at the Musée de l'Elysée in Lausanne, Switzerland.

In India, Daniélou divided his time between Santiniketan, Varanasi, Almora, Chennai and Pondicherry. He met and worked with Rabindranath Tagore and became the director of the School of Music at Tagore's Visva Bharati (World University) at Santiniketan. Well-versed in western music, he took up the study of Indian music and was appointed professor at the Banaras Hindu University in 1949, and later the director of the College of Indian Music.

In 1960, he worked on the UNESCO collection, a series of recordings of traditional world music. He also founded the International Institute for Comparative Music Studies and Documentation in Berlin and Venice. Recognised for his work, he received, among other awards, the UNESCO/CIM prize for music in 1981 and in 1991 a Fellowship from the Sangeet Natak Akademi in India.

The Santal comprise the single largest tribal community in India. Though spread across the eastern states—Jharkhand, West Bengal, Odisha, Bihar and beyond—they yet form a distinct geography and culture.

The Santal are best known outside their community for their rich traditions of dance and music, especially the latter, which has influenced mainstream music in India. Their attitude of respect and care of the environment and the status and freedoms of Santal women have also, over many years, been noted and admired.

Their cultural influence, while pervasive, has never been insistent. Perhaps this is because others have taken from their traditions what they wanted and the community itself has had neither the inclination nor the opportunity to market its talents and resources. Certainly, despite their large numbers, the Santal have received less exposure than many other tribal traditions, and are not present in the same way in the consciousness of people or in the arena of commerce in the contemporary world.

But the Santal community has been extensively documented for more than a century. Their very distinct culture has attracted researchers, scholars, travellers and explorers into their midst, who have brought back Santal stories and objects.

This book is one of the outcomes of a collaborative project between the Museum Rietberg, Zurich, and the Crafts Museum, New Delhi, a partnership that was, in a sense, sparked off by a collection of Santal musical instruments recently donated to the Museum Rietberg and shown in an exhibition inaugurated there in September 2014. Bengt Fosshag, the collector and donor, is a Graphic Designer from Germany. He is also an amateur musician, and had been collecting Santal instruments since the late 1960s. He chose them for aesthetic reasons, because he appreciated their craftsmanship and found them attractive and interesting objects.

Over the past few years, Museum Rietberg has expanded its attention to the tribal arts of India, a subject that has not really been its focus over the last few decades. Bronzes, textiles and most recently, musical instruments, have been acquired through private collectors who have entrusted the Museum Rietberg with the collections they built up over the second half of the 20th century.

The intention of the Museum Rietberg in extending its collection is to document these unique tribal traditions and raise public awareness about them. In this way cultural traditions which may be at risk of disappearing can be preserved for posterity, even if within a museal context. Our modest aim is the care and maintenance, documentation and display of the artefacts, as also of the intangible heritage associated with them.

Contact between the objects of a particular culture, and people of another finds echoes across the centuries, through the colonial period and much beyond. The desire to know and engage with distant countries and cultures has often been expressed through the enduring fascination with the objects of the 'Other'. The tradition of collecting has meant also that such objects of passion have voyaged to distant lands and there been carefully preserved. Pointing to the importance of 'things'[1], it encourages us to consider how an object is born, how it is held, how it disperses, how, passing through many hands, it gains stories and its significance changes, alongside its changing and deepening patina. No less significant, though more intangible, is how the object may have affected those who came into contact with it, chose it, knew it, and cared for it, through its various transits.

The present collaborative project allows us to revisit some of these objects and traditions to discover missing links and enable the further documentation of tangible and intangible heritage. In this, the various activities of the Crafts Museum have been invaluable. Through its Research and Documentation Programme the Crafts Museum supports research projects in crafts documentation and a detailed report prepared under this programme on Santal Puppetry is published here for the first time. The Crafts Demonstration Programme is another important initiative of the Crafts Museum where craftspeople are invited from different parts of the country to be in residence for a month at 'Shilpa Kuteer', the artists' residence at the museum. Through this programme we were able to invite craftsmen and performers of the Santal community to the museum, to interact with them and carry out the research and documentation for the present project.

The book brings together the material collected in this project, and so essentially records *this* moment in the history of the documentation of the Santal community. Through the conversations with the craftsmen at the Crafts Demonstration Programme, we have tried to convey their views and observations that are, perforce, based on this very small sample. These are offered more as vignettes than any claim to generality, offering a flavour or a snapshot of their particular experience. It is remarkable that the craftsmen with whom we interacted in 2014 were the same craftsmen interviewed in 1988. The same researcher was also present in the two interactions. Therefore there is a valid comparison in their responses and reactions to their changing world. What seems to emerge from the several contributions is that while many traditions survive, various factors are affecting their form and manifestation. Earlier rhythms continue, but haltingly, and increasingly face the contrasting beats and vibrations of a rapidly changing surrounding reality.

We take this opportunity to thank all those involved in the production of this book. The enterprise has included the contributions of people of very varied ages, background, countries and expertise, and the synergy has been exceptional. We hope the book will be enjoyed by as diverse an audience.

Ruchira Ghose, Crafts Museum, New Delhi, India
Albert Lutz, Museum Rietberg, Zurich, Switzerland

New Delhi and Zurich, January 2015

1 Edmund de Waal (2001) in *The Hare with the Amber Eyes*, talks of this in context of Netsuke, miniature Japanese sculptures, traditionally used as toggles, which have been handed down through the generations.

# INTRODUCTION

Johannes Beltz
Marie-Eve Celio-Scheurer

The present publication represents an Indo-Swiss joint venture between the Crafts Museum in New Delhi and the Museum Rietberg in Zurich. It is the result of an ongoing cooperation project in the field of research, curating and design and is connected to two exhibitions related to the Santal: one titled 'Sculpted Sound: Stringed Instruments from India' at the Museum Rietberg, Zurich, and one titled 'Cadence and Counterpoint: Documenting Santal Musical Traditions' at the National Museum, New Delhi.

## THE BENGT FOSSHAG COLLECTION

To understand the dynamics and implications of the project one has to go back to November 2013 when the Museum Rietberg acquired an outstanding collection of 92 stringed instruments, largely of South Asian origin. The collection was partly donated by, and partly bought from, a German collector, Bengt Fosshag. This is an interesting story in itself. Bengt Fosshag never travelled to South Asia, but acquired his entire collection from dealers in Europe. He worked from 1960–1970 as Art Director for several advertising agencies and as Designer for the Opel GM factory in Rüsselsheim. From 1971–1983 he ran his own creative studio, SIGN, and since has worked as a freelance graphic designer and illustrator for German advertising agencies, reputed magazines, newspapers and publishing houses.

Some years ago he started to look for a safe place to house his collections. He approached some ethnographic museums in Germany but they were reluctant to take up his offer. Perhaps they were anxious about the price of the acquisition or the cost of its long-term preservation. But when Bengt Fosshag approached the Museum Rietberg, we saw a unique opportunity to enhance the museum collection. We also understood the Bengt Fosshag collection needed to be preserved in its entirety and should not be split up and dispersed through dealers and auctions. Our thoughts and concerns were shared with the Rietberg-Kreis, a circle of sponsors who gladly acquired a large part of the collection. Bengt Fosshag offered the remaining part as a donation. Without the support of these generous friends we could not have acquired the collection.

## COLLECTING TRIBAL INSTRUMENTS IN AN ART MUSEUM

The collection marks a recent development in the history of the Museum Rietberg. Earlier, the Rietberg would have been reluctant to collect Indian objects of relatively recent origin which one might label 'craft' rather than 'art'. The museum was founded as a museum of non-European art in 1952. The founding collector Eduard von der Heydt (1882–1964) and its first director Johannes Itten (1888–1967), conceptualized the museum of formal art, rather than an ethnographic museum, which already existed in Zurich in the form of the Völkerkunde Museum.

The mission of the Rietberg was to collect and exhibit world art. The guiding principle was that truly universal art exists above all national or geographic boundaries; that there exists a universal aesthetic, which could be applied across countries and cultures.

Following this idea, the Rietberg exhibited its collection of art from around the world in classic European museum style; like Greek sculpture, Indian bronzes were displayed on mounts, presented as masterpieces with a certain 'aura', and placed in large gallery spaces. This presentation differed significantly from the typical ethnographic museum of the time, which displayed objects referencing their original contexts with maps, photographs and elaborate explanations.

The Museum Rietberg kept to its original mandate over several decades and today the Rietberg name is associated with excellence, both in the breadth of its collections and their display. The museum also emphasises the importance of the individual artist. It became the commitment of subsequent generations of directors and curators not just to attribute but also to identify paintings and sculptures to specific artists. Artworks were not only representative of a local style, a historic period, an ethnic community; masterpieces in the true sense of the term reveal as well profound individual talent, knowledge, craftsmanship and creativity.

Significantly, the founding collector, Eduard von der Heydt, collected only 'classical' Indian art, such as South Indian Chola bronzes and sculptures. However, he never travelled to India, buying art only from international art dealers. Also he did not buy any contemporary Indian 'tribal' art.[1]

The Museum Rietberg continued to collect for some time within this category of 'high' art. This specialisation is also a consequence of the differentiation, even competition, between ethnographic and art museums. While ethnographic museums collected objects of daily use, most of them of recent origin, art museums focussed on unique masterpieces. As such, the Museum Rietberg would typically not acquire sculptures, bronzes or textiles that were recently made. The label 'masterpiece' was applied only to antique and expensive objects, preferably sold at established art galleries.

It was the former director Eberhard Fischer (b. 1941) who challenged this dichotomy and produced a series of exhibitions on Indian art, which presented not only courtly paintings but also representations of tribal and folk art. It was his ambition to enlarge the notion of Indian art while including other marginalized traditions.[2] We would like to mention here the exemplary exhibition on arts and crafts of Odisha, which presented works of artists in the fields of weaving, wood-carving, pottery, wall painting, manuscript illustration and architecture. As a curator, however, Eberhard Fischer expanded his collection most of all in the field of miniature painting. A significant shift took place only after his successor joined the Museum Rietberg. An important collection of south Indian Bhuta masks was acquired in 2008, followed by several collections of Bastar bronzes. After his retirement, Eberhard Fischer himself donated his collection of modern textiles from Gujarat to the museum. All these donations were well documented and accompanied by several exhibitions and catalogues.[3]

Since then the Museum Rietberg has expanded its focus by collecting not only Indian tribal art but also Chinese propaganda photographs. It offers a rich and attractive menu of exhibitions: comparative shows on mysticism, erotic art, cosmologies and comics. The Rietberg is today a museum of world cultures.

## COOPERATION WITH THE CRAFTS MUSEUM, NEW DELHI

It is a practice at the Rietberg that major new acquisitions are published and celebrated through an exhibition and an accompanying catalogue. This is the museum's commitment and gesture of gratitude towards the donor and fulfils its duty to make its collections accessible. Within less than a year of the acquisition, the exhibition 'Sculpted Sound: Stringed instruments from India' was opened on 4 September 2014.

While unpacking and documenting the instruments of the Bengt Fosshag collection, we were particularly struck by the sculptural Santal stringed instruments called *Banam*: the 44 pieces of this category represent the single largest group of the collection. The exquisitely carved and decorated *Banam* tell us about the high level of sculpting skills of the Santal as well as their particular motifs and icons. As we admired the instruments, we wondered about their iconography. We were also curious to know more about the people who made or used these instruments.

This desire to better understand the objects led us to initiate a collaborative project with Crafts Museum in India based on an exchange of knowledge and competences. For European museums with collections of non-European art, such collaborations are the only way to legitimize their existence and to flourish in a globalized world.[4] It is critical today to create links between museums and experts, between objects and their origin—links that go beyond geographical and cultural borders—in order to preserve and valorise world heritage.

In this sense the cooperation with the Crafts Museum is a pioneering Swiss-Indo cooperation project which is much more significant than it might at first appear. This cooperation not only allows a knowledge transfer in both directions, Indian and Swiss, but also provides an opportunity for both the Rietberg and the Crafts Museum to connect to the communities from which the objects and traditions originate.

The collaboration project between the Museum Rietberg and the Crafts Museum is supported by the Swiss Federal Office of Culture, the Embassy of Switzerland in India and UNESCO (India).

## PRESERVATION OF TANGIBLE AND INTANGIBLE HERITAGE

One of the shortcomings of the Rietberg exhibition was that the instruments, for obvious reasons, could not be played. Also concerts or rituals could not be performed in the exhibition space. While the audio and video installations gave the audience some idea of the variety of practices associated with these instruments, they remained distanced from their living practice. This is not a trivial issue. In recent years the museum world has foregrounded the issue of intangible heritage: the necessity to preserve not just material culture but also immaterial culture. As the terms suggest, tangible is what we can touch, intangible is what we say or hear or do.[5]

Tangible and intangible heritage are inextricably intertwined and this is best seen with musical instruments. An exhibition like the one at the Rietberg highlights the visual and sculptural beauty of the instruments. But what about the community that makes these instruments? What about its musical traditions? How are the instruments made and what is the music that emanates from them?

From its inception, the Crafts Museum has been concerned with the preservation and valorisation of folk and tribal arts. In fact, tribal traditions represent some of the richest in crafts skills and the Santal are probably the oldest, certainly the largest, tribal population in India. The Crafts Museum, moreover, offers a unique residency programme to which artists, craftsmen, performers, dancers, musicians are invited, thus making the museum an invaluable site for the research and documentation of tangible and intangible heritage.

## THE EXHIBITION

The idea behind the collaborative effort was to take forward the initiative of the Museum Rietberg by combining expertise and resources across the two countries. We were keen to produce an original exhibition about the musical traditions of the Santal, reflecting both their tangible and intangible living heritage.

The exhibition will be held at the National Museum in April 2015, and has been curated by the Museum Rietberg and the Crafts Museum. The exhibition design has been done by Kanu Kartik Agrawal, Architect and Designer based in New Delhi. Pierre Girardin and Philippe Karrer, from ECAL/University of Art and Design Lausanne, Switzerland, have contributed graphic design elements. Mushtak Khan and Krittika Narula at the Crafts Museum have looked after the research and documentation.

The exhibition in New Delhi will present three types of objects linked to the Santal musical tradition: the instruments themselves, with the *Banam* in particular, but also two types of drums called *Tamak* and *Madal*; the *Chadar Badar* puppetry of the Santal community; and the *Jadupatua*, or scroll paintings. Significantly, given the focus on intangible heritage, the exhibition will include previously unpublished and rare materials from various archives — photographs, films, songs (including recordings from 1914) and primary research.

## THE PUBLICATION

This publication is a follow up to the German catalogue *Klang Körper: Saiteninstrumente aus Indien* which accompanied the exhibition held at the Rietberg. For the Santal exhibition at New Delhi, the publication needed to be enlarged. Thanks are due to the Accentus Foundation and Elena Probst Fonds for their generous support which enabled us to prepare this publication in English.

Bengt Fosshag explains how he became interested in collecting Santal instruments and what fascinated him most. Ludwig Pesch, musicologist and flute player, writes on Santal music, influences and evolutions. Jayasri Banerjee, musicologist and sitar player, who has done field research among the Santal, offers an essay on the musical tradition of the Santal and recent developments. Marine Carrin, an ethnologist who has lived among the Santal, offers an essay on the *Baha* (flowers) festival. Ravi Kant Dwivedi, a pioneer in the documentation of Santal traditions writes on *Chadar Badar* puppetry. Mushtak Khan, Krittika Narula and Mallika Leuzinger have compiled the report of Ravi Kant Dwivedi's field trip in 2014 and recorded the conversations with the Santal craftsmen and women on a variety of topics.

The design of the book has been a collaborative venture: Malini Saigal, the Editor of the book in New Delhi has worked with Designers Philippe Karrer and Pierre Girardin from ECAL.

*Cadence and Counterpoint: Documenting Santal Musical Traditions* makes no claim other than raising awareness and respect of Santal musical heritage — a heritage which travelled from India to Europe and captured the imagination of a German collector, and eventually found its home at the Museum Rietberg in Switzerland. The search for knowledge about these musical instruments led to a journey back to India, to the Crafts Museum, a remarkable and fecund site of intangible heritage.

1 See the first systematic research on this extraordinary individual, collector, donator and banker: Illner, 2013.
2 Eberhard Fischer, Haku Shah, *Kunsttraditionen in Nordindien. Stammeskunst, Volkskunst, klassische Kunst*, Böblingen, Codex Verlag, 1972; Eberhard Fischer, Sitakant Mahapatra, Dinanath Pathy (eds.), *Orissa: Kunst und Kultur in Nordost-Indien*, Zurich, Museum Rietberg, 1980.
3 Johannes Beltz (ed.), *Wenn Masken tanzen, Rituelles Theater und Bronzekunst aus Südindien*, Zurich, Museum Rietberg, 2009; Johannes Beltz, Cornelia Mallebrein (eds.), *Elefanten, schaukelnde Götter und Tänzer in Trance: Bronzekunst aus dem heutigen Indien*, Zurich, Museum Rietberg, 2012; Eberhard Fischer, Jyotindra Jain, Haku Shah, *Temple Tents for the Goddesses in Gujarat, India*, New Delhi, Niyogi Books, 2013.
4 See in particular Raymond A. Silverman (ed.), *Museum as Process. Translating Local and Global Knowledges*, London, Routledge, 2015.
5 See for example Laurajane Smith and Natsuko Akagawa (eds.), *Intangible Heritage*, London, Routledge, 2009.

# PHOTOGRAPHS FROM 1973

## Deben Bhattacharya

Deben Bhattacharya (1921–2001) took these photographs in January 1973 while travelling in the Santal village of Kamarbaudi (District Midnapore). They are a selection from the 162 slides he prepared with comments[1] that are kept in the Bhattacharya private archives in Paris and Kolkata owned by his wife, Jharna Bose Bhattacharya. Part of the archives is also housed in the Sound Archives of the Bibliothèque nationale de France in Paris. The photographer Brenda Turnnidge has digitized the slides and comments.

Deben Bhattacharya was a Bengali musicologist, record producer, documentary filmmaker and writer who, when not on his frequent travels on work, lived in Kolkata and Paris. He produced over 130 records and 20 films of the music cultures of 30 countries of Asia, Middle East and Europe and published more than a dozen books. Much of his work was carried out under the auspices of UNESCO. From his large body of work, two documents on the Santal community have been released: one documentary film, *Faces of the Forest* (DVD, 1973, 27 minutes) and one musical album, *Music of the Santal Tribe* (CD, recorded in 1954 and 1973, released in 2014).

1 Deben Bhattacharya comments on these images as follows: "Santal village life, architecture, water well, (...)" (p.29, 31 below, 33); "Santal face"(p. 30); "Straw peacock in the front field of a village house to mark the area of dance'" (p. 31 above); "Polishing of the clay huts" (p. 32); "*Dunger Enech*, Santal hunting dance with *Shankoya* (buffalo horn) and several *Tamak* (large kettle drum beaten with 2 sticks)" (p. 40, 41 above); "*Banam*, Santal fiddle with single string and hunter's bow" (p. 35 below); "*Lhuri Jhika*, dance for the end of day's work. Accompanying instruments: 2 *Tamaks* (...) and 2 *Madals* (barrel drums played with hands)" (p. 34, 36); "*Tukhda* (*Madal*), Santal barrel drum, played with both hands" (p. 38); "*Tiriyo*, Santal transverse bamboo flute (6 finger holes)" (p. 37).

# BUILDING THE COLLECTION[1]



Bengt Fosshag

The story of my collection begins in the late 1960s, when Heinz von zur Mühlen, an old school friend of mine, brought me back a *Sarinda* from Lahore, Pakistan, which he called 'Skull-*Sarinda*'. The violin-like instrument with its two big sound holes did indeed bring to mind the skull of a dead animal. This gift marked the beginning of my love for these stringed instruments.

## TENTATIVE BEGINNINGS

This instrument first inspired me to acquaint myself with the literature surrounding foreign stringed instruments. I visited an exhibition at the Münchner Stadtmuseum of beautiful non-European stringed instruments, taken from a private collection, and it was then that my fascination developed into a wish to acquire such pieces myself. But where was I to begin, where could I buy such instruments? I could not find them at auctions. Nor did I know any specialised dealers. So I started to bring stringed instruments back with me from trips to Turkey and Morocco. Friends who knew about my weakness contributed one or other piece. These were mostly simple instruments that could be purchased cheaply on vacation. At the time, I had no strategy — I simply bought what I liked! Yet in hindsight, I think of it as an incredibly exciting time.

On one occasion, a former colleague at Opel gifted me a small, very delicate Turkish *Kemenche* that he had built himself. He did not have a genuine Turkish instrument at home, and as he desperately wanted to own and play one, he simply produced one himself His craftsmanship was really excellent and the only thing he lacked in fabrication was the right piece of wood. He made do with wood which was available in his department of the Opel plant, but which was very narrow: as a result, his instrument was quite narrow but nonetheless playable, even if the sound was somewhat thin. When somebody brought him an original instrument from Turkey, he gifted me his self-made "emergency solution".

On another occasion, I was able to procure a lyre from Greece through my neighbour, a Greek hairstylist. These instruments are a little shrill and are played at breakneck speed, which, in a German rented flat, can frustrate fellow occupants and neighbours. This was also why a second lyre slipped through my fingers: the long-suffering wife of a neighbour who was a lyre-player smashed the instrument to pieces in a fit of anger. Finally, an acquaintance brought me a *Tar* and a dulcimer from Iran. What I bought at the time constituted a veritable smorgasbord that cut right across the variety of string instruments. But nestled within it were several interesting pieces.

## THE LUTE COLLECTION

It soon became clear to me that I would have to limit my collection to one type of instrument if I wanted to maintain a meaningful coherence. In my eyes, lutes form the most interesting group of stringed instruments, because they are the most diverse. There are spike lutes and necked lutes, long-necked and short-necked lutes, bowl lutes and box lutes with wood or skin coverings. As I began to collect systematically, I was initially only interested in having one example of each type. I obviously wanted to procure objects that could also be shown in a museum, but I had hardly any connections to good dealers, which made it difficult to find good pieces. With time this changed, and I was able to procure more and more antique and high-quality instruments. I was in awe of these objects. I learnt how one could perceive the changes wrought by use on these old, much-used instruments. The fingers of the left hand always press the strings onto the same points of the neck, so that little dips form and the back of the neck becomes polished as the hand moves up and down it. The smokey surface created by the chimney-less firing in Indian and Nepalese households gives the instruments a shining black or brownish surface. One instrument in the collection has a coat of rust that is as thick as those one finds on sacrificial sculptures from Western Nepal.

The lute works like a guitar, an instrument I have long known and loved, and have avidly played since around 1960. It was therefore especially interesting for me to compare the designs of these two instruments. Lutes have a sound box, which amplifies the vibrations of the strings that are transferred to the top by a bridge. The strings need to be attached to the body and tuned. They have to stretch across the neck over a particular distance, the neck in turn making it possible to shorten the strings to the desired pitch.

This mechanism for producing notes is the same for all lutes. Their forms, however, are very varied. Materials, technical details and cultural differences are at the root of this diversity. I have described and illustrated the technical details in the catalogue *Kunstwerk and Werkzeug*[2] which accompanied the exhibition of the same name in the Historisches Museum Frankfurt. I sketched the development of the *Rabab* instruments under the title 'The Sarinda and its Relatives'[3] for the *Journal for the History of Arab-Islamic Studies*.[4] To get to grips with the characteristics of the instruments, I stuck photographs into sketchbooks and annotated them.

## *DHODRO BANAM*: THE INSTRUMENT AS SCULPTURE

The Frankfurt exhibition displayed several instruments that fascinated me above all because of their sculptural beauty. These were the Santal lutes. These instruments drove me to redirect the focus of my collection. I no longer collected simply lute instruments, but lute sculptures. What was especially noteworthy for me was the disarming similarity these objects had to African art, something which, time and again, led people to characterise me as a collector. In reality, however, they were the artwork of an Adivasi community, namely the Santals. In an article entitled 'The Lutes of the Santal' written for the art journal *Tribal Arts* (1996), I described what was known about these instruments. That same year, I donated a large part of my collection to the Linden-Museum in Stuttgart for the exhibition 'Mit Haut und Haar'. Thereafter, I concentrated only on the Santal instrument *Dhodro Banam* and the Nepalese *Damyen*. Over the years I was able to acquire numerous extremely interesting examples of *Rabab* lutes to which the above-mentioned types belong.

## MY APPROACH TO COLLECTING

A collector often tends to procure only prize pieces (whatever that may be). But one can also add ordinary objects to a collection, insofar as they are interesting. It seems to me that, above all, it is the principle behind the collection, that is to say a specific attitude toward collecting, that is important for a collection. I decided that my collection should include instruments from first-rate instrument makers alongside those made by amateurs or musicians with a flair for handcrafting. I wanted to present the full range of artistic creation.

Many owners decorated their instrument with metal and synthetic materials, or carved a new pattern onto the head of the instrument. The way in which the instrument could be played was also always re-adjusted according to their needs. Some instrument makers attempted to imitate the instruments of higher castes in what could be called a musical confidence trick! It is precisely these self-made or modified instruments that interest me because they make visible the intimate relationship between musician and instrument.

The representation of figures on the head of the instrument seems to be connected to seasonal festivals and special occasions, for they constantly depict scenes of music and dance. Older, more valuable lutes portray groups of dancers with musicians in a stylistically similar manner, which leads me to surmise that they must all belong to the same workshop. The British ethnologist Verrier Elwin had already collected similar instruments in the 1950s—it is this variation on the same subject that makes collecting so exciting for me.

## SCHOLARS AND DEALERS

To deepen my knowledge I sought out not just literature about non-European lute instruments, but also the help of people with knowledge of the field. I would like to particularly mention Wolf Dietrich, a computer specialist; Ursula Reinhard and her husband Kurt, the director of the Institut für Vergleichende Musikwissenschaft[5] in Berlin; and the music ethnologist and professor Artur Simon, who introduced me to the musical instruments. Thanks to my contact with Dr. Reimund Vogels and Prof. Lars-Christian Koch, I was able to participate in the publication of the accompanying text for the Lute exhibition 'Mit Haut und Haar' in the Linden-Museum Stuttgart in 1996. Professor Ricardo Eichmann, the first director of the Oriental department of the Deutsche Archäologisches Institut[6] supported me as a lute-enthusiast, music archaeologist and expert whose sensitive and detailed illustrations gave me much joy. If I remember correctly, I came to know him through Dr. Klaus Peter Brenner, the curator of the musical instrument collection at the University of Göttingen where I was able to study several very interesting pieces from Afghanistan and Nepal. Dr. Walter Limberg had published a book on land ownership and field cultivation amongst Sherpas and was kind enough to provide me with photographs of the lute maker Mingma Lama.

After a lifetime of collecting, one inevitably gets to know dealers who can supply the much yearned-for pieces. Lothar Heubel's antique store on Frankfurt's Braubachstrasse, which sold art objects from India and Nepal, was a cabinet of curiosities for me. Here I could occasionally find Indian *Sarangis* and Afghan *Rababs*. It was here that small black lutes with horses' heads suddenly appeared in the 1980s. I thought that they must be forgeries, as I could find no mention of similar objects in any of the literature. In 1981, the Ile du Demon Gallery in Paris brought out a small book that featured a couple of these *Damyen*. It was only in 1990, however, that the booklet fell into my hands. It was in Lothar Heubel's headquarters in Cologne that many Indian instruments were to be found. In Frankfurt, I later discovered another source: the import business Sedig, where one could acquire various Afghan lutes alongside furniture.

One day in the late 1980s, a stranger laden with two heavy bags in which I could make out musical instruments, hurried past me on the way to one of Munich's flea markets. It later emerged that these instruments were *Dhodro Banams*. I had learnt about them through Verrier Elwin's publications but this was my first encounter with them. From 1991 onwards François Pannier offered numerous examples of this type in his Galerie Le Toit du Monde in Paris. I came to know this dealer of Himalayan Art through a friend who was travelling through Paris and was familiar with my collection. She took a photograph of a *Dhodro Banam* and brought it to me. The negotiations between dealers and buyers were rather difficult in those pre-email years. Every communication was carried out via photographs and through the post. On 17 May 1991 Pannier sent out invitations to a preview of an exhibition of Santal lutes and it was such a pleasure to see other Santal lutes!

In the 1980s, there was a trend among certain European travellers to India and Pakistan to earn a living selling indigenous objects in Europe. Amongst them was Jörn Raeck, whom I found through a newspaper advertisement. He was a throat singer and sold bagpipes and other musical instruments. Through him I became acquainted with the gallerist Lambert Abraham from Düsseldorf. The quality of the Santal lutes available on the antique market around 1990 is clearly visible in photographs. Later, forgeries abounded. At a trade fair in Frankfurt I came across Tudi Billo, who runs a Nepalese import business in Nordhessen. Nestled amongst cheap goods were some extremely lovely pieces. In the 1990s I also forged relationships with several galleries in Brussels, London and Paris.

## THE LUTES ARRIVE IN GERMANY

To my knowledge Santal lutes are seldom put up for auction since they tend to be spontaneously purchased for their original appearance and not collected as, for instance, are African harps. Often it is artists, or the artistically inclined, that most appreciate these strange sculptures.

A few decades ago, all manner of goods including Santal lutes were imported en masse from Nepal. It wasn't long before many counterfeits were also on their way. An acquaintance told me how, in 1991, a dealer would telephone him and a German artist every time a new shipment arrived, whereupon they collected many beautiful pieces from the container. The instruments—also included in these shipments—thus made their way to dealers who, in turn, passed them on to instrument-lovers.

As a child I had enthusiastically leafed through travel books; later I became interested in European artists who drew inspiration from African artists. I was equally excited by music from foreign countries, which was not all that easy to find in the late 1950s. Each of the instruments collected here has enriched my knowledge and allowed me to make new discoveries. With each I have formed a very particular and unique relationship, and I remember the stories and people that connect to it. This, for me, is something extremely valuable.

1 Translated from German to English by Mallika Leuzinger.
2 Dietrich und Fosshag, 1992.
3 'Die Sarinda und Ihre Verwandten' *Zeitschrift für Geschichte der Aarabisch-Iislamischen Wissenschaften*, Universität Frankfurt am Main, 1997.
4 *Ibid.*
5 Institute of Comparative Music Study, Berlin.
6 The German Institute of Archaeology, Berlin.

Bengt Fosshag's stringed instruments as displayed in his home at Rüsselsheim, November 2012

The story begins in 1968, with the gift of a stringed instrument.[1] Bengt Fosshag, the collector and donor, describes in his essay how the gift of this instrument from a friend became the starting point of a collection he would assemble over several decades until its donation to the Museum Rietberg in 2013.[2]

The collection comprises 92 musical instruments; all but nine come from India and Nepal.[3] Most were made in the first part of the twentieth century. Wood is the primary material, but the instruments are sometimes decorated with ivory, bone, metal, glass, mother of pearl and bamboo. Several instruments show traces of pigment. The cover of the sound box is made from animal skin (usually reptile, cow or goat). Other strings made from animal hide, gut, metal or plastic are likely replacements necessitated by wear and tear.[4] Few bows have survived, as have few bridges on the instruments.[5]

The instruments all belong to the chordophone family.[6] Bengt Fosshag assigned his instruments to particular categories and gave a classification that we have adopted. According to this classification, the collection is divided into two groups. The first consists of stringed instruments played with a bow—two *Sarangi* instruments[7], 17 *Sarinda* instruments[8] and the large group of Santal instruments with six *Huka Banam*[9] and 38 *Dhodro Banam*[10] which are of special sculptural quality. The second group is formed of plucked string instruments, including 18 *Damyen*[11] and two *Dotara*[12]. Some instruments in the collection could be classified under either category, since they are both plucked and played with a bow. The seven *Rababs*[13] in the collection belong to this group.

## SANTAL STRINGED INSTRUMENTS

A conclusive classification of *Banam* instruments remains elusive because of the multiple features that need to be recorded, such as structure and decorative elements. Bengt Fosshag distinguishes two types of *Banam*: one with neck at top, the other with neck at bottom. The most popular are the *Dhodro Banam* ('hollow instrument') and *Huka Banam* ('coconut instrument').

The *Dhodro Banam* is usually made from a single piece of wood[14] sectioned into four parts.[15] The *Banam* maker begins with the carving of the stomach (*lac*), which is hollowed out in an oval shape. The chest (*koram*) is also hollowed out and is attached to the stomach as a rectangle; the neck (*hotok*) is straight and leads into the head (*bohok*). The lower part of the head has a hole for the string, which is attached to the ear (*lutur*) or key. The stomach of the instrument is then covered with animal skin. Strings are made of goat gut and fastened onto a wooden bridge (*sadom*). The bow (*banam ak*) is traditionally made with horse hair, but sometimes also with buffalo hair, jute or tree fibre[16].

The *Dhodro Banam* usually has just one string which appears out of the 'mouth' of the instrument. Just as its shape resembles the human form, so its sound, the human voice. The sculpted figures on the instrument are often human or animal, sometimes both. The instruments are played with the bow held in the right hand while the left hand holds the instrument vertically and is turned to face the audience. According to the British ethnologist, Verrier Elwin (1902–1964), the instrument was principally played by *yogis* or wandering ascetics. It used to be said that if the musician died, his instrument was cremated with him. But the age of the instruments in the collection, the signs of intensive use and visible repairs, suggest this custom was not strictly followed.

## SCULPTED SOUND

These instruments make up a unique collection, rich in form and meaning. Further exploration of the associated intangible and tangible heritage will deepen our experience and understanding of the instruments as also of the communities from which they have emerged.

1 This instrument belongs now to the Museum Rietberg, Inv. No. 2014.17.
2 *Ibid.*
3 These are: Museum Rietberg, Inv. No. 2014.11 (*Rabab* from Yemen), 2014.12 (*Rabab* from Morocco), 2014.13 (*Rabab* from Zanskar), 2014.17 (*Sarinda* from Pakistan), 2014.18 (*Sarinda* from Afghanistan), 2014.73 and 74 (*Rababs* from Afghanistan), 2014.79 (*Sarinda* probably from Burma) and 2014.92 (*Damyen* probably from Bhutan).
4 Strings are still present on 33 instruments: Museum Rietberg, Inv. No. 2014.9–18, 2014.25, 2014.32, 2014.34, 2014.37, 2014.38, 2014.47, 2014.59, 2014.66, 2014.68–73, 2014.78, 2014.79, 2014.82–85, 2014.90, 2014.92.
5 The following 15 instruments still have their bridge, even though not always original: Museum Rietberg, Inv. No. 2014.9, 2014.11, 2014.12, 2014.15–18, 2014.34, 2014.37, 2014.38, 2014.73, 2014.78, 2014.79, 2014.82, 2014.84.
6 About the classification of the musical instruments see, among others: Tranchefort, 1980. About the origin myth of the fiddle, see: http://médiatheque.cite-musique.fr.
7 The two *Sarangi* are: Museum Rietberg, Inv. No. 2014.16 and 2014.34.
8 The 17 *Sarinda*, also called *Sorud*, *Surando*, *Saro*, are: Museum Rietberg, Inv. No. 2014.14, 2014.15, 2014.17, 2014.18, 2014.29–33, 2014.75–82.
9 The six *Huka Banam* are: Museum Rietberg, Inv. No. 2014.10, 2014.20–22, 2014.94, and 2014.95.
10 The 38 *Dhodro Banam* are: Museum Rietberg, Inv. No. 2014.5–9, 2014.19, 2014.23–28, 2014.35, 2014.36, 2014.42–65.
11 The 18 *Damyen*, also called *Damjen*, *Dramyien*, *Dranyen*, *Dramnyen* or *Sgra-Snyan*, are: Museum Rietberg, Inv. No. 2014.41, 2014.66–72, 2014.83–92.
12 The two *Dotara* or *Kasi Duitara*, are: Museum Rietberg, Inv. No. 2014.37 and 2014.38.
13 The seven *Rabab*, or *Rubab*, *Roubab*, *Robab*, *Rebab*, *Rubob*, *Rawap*, are: Museum Rietberg, Inv. No. 2014.11–13, 2014.39, 2014.73, 2014.74, and 2014.96.
14 According to Ravi Kant Dwivedi who interviewed the Santal artists at the Crafts Museum, New Delhi, in December 2014, the *Banam* is made from the wood of the tree called *Guloj*, also known as *Champa* or the Indian Temple Tree. *Plumeria Obtusa* is the botanical name. It is a small tree famous for its scented white flowers with pale yellow centres, and its wood is supposed to give a sound sweeter than others.
15 About the *Banam*, see also: Onkar Prasad, *Santal Music*, 1985, p. 100–106.
16 Bhulu Murmu, Santal artist, provided this information.

# ON SANTAL MUSIC AND MUSICAL INSTRUMENTS

Jayasri Banerjee

This essay explores the unique musical tradition of the Santals living in the forest lands or Jungle Mahal, in West Bengal. The Santals are an indigenous people, who inhabit these areas and make a living through agriculture and the use of forest resources. They are well known for their distinctive *seren-enec* or song-dance traditions.

I would like to clarify at the outset that I consider Santal musical traditions as unique not because of any romantic vision of their primordial and pristine way of life, unaffected by modernity but rather because of its very specific musical elements: intonation pattern, rhythmic structure and metric frame, as well as aesthetic principles. Also unique is the manner in which this tradition manifests as an intimate relationship between song, dance, musical instruments, language, performance, in the context of landscape and socialization. The system of transmission of musical knowledge of the Santal, through a collective oral-aural and participative method, is also distinct.

Jungle Mahal, which literally means 'forest region', represents an interesting crossover between reality and imagination. It exists neither in the recent maps of Burdwan or Birbhum Districts, nor in the current files of the District Administrations. Once synonymous with rebellion, sedition and unrest against colonial power and local landlords, the boundaries of Jungle Mahal were changed to suit the administrative needs of the state. Over time the term Jungle Mahal disappeared from official vocabulary only to briefly reappear in the 1970s, interestingly enough, in the context of the ultra left Naxalite movement. But Jungle Mahal is very much alive in the memories of the Santals: it is still there in their festivals of *Sohrai* and *Baha, Dasae* and *Karam*, in their songs and dances, in their rites and rituals, in their *Jaher Than* (Sacred Grove), and in the everyday presence of *Marang Buru* (the mountain god) and *Pilchu Haram* and *Pilchu Budhi* (first man and first woman of the Santal), and innumerable *Bongas* (spirits). Jungle Mahal is still there in the oral narratives of the people. It is not a mere geographical location but also a cultural space.

In this complex texture of past and present are located Santal musical traditions. Through the celebration of their festivals for which they have specific songs, dances and musical instruments, they look back to an earlier way of life which centred around nature, their sacred forest and the ancestors.

*Sal* (*Shorea robusta*) forest in Jungle Mahal, 1999

## THE MELODIC STRUCTURE

These musical instruments form the base for the distinct character of Santal musical traditions. The melodic structure of the music is based on its unique intonation pattern. For example, the second note of their musical 'scale', that is *Ri*, is slightly flatter than the one ordinarily used. Also, the melodic movement of this music is marked by a gradual undulation or traverse across the finer intervals between two notes and not by a sharp leap from one pitch point to another. In Santal music, melody and language are integrated and multiple song texts set in a limited number of genre-specific melodic constructs. The social linguist Nishant Choksi has highlighted this integral relationship: "In Santali, ordinary human speech (*rod'*) and melodic sung speech (*ra.d*) are seen on a continuum, with *ra.d'* seen as a natural extension of *rod'*."[2] Referring to the text-tune relationship in Santal music, Onkar Prasad points out that tune or melody "provides structural values to its text."

*Sakhrat Parav*: returning home after hunting, 1999

Details of the number of lines in a song text and/or what would be the length of each line in such text, are largely determined by tune (that is, melody). In Santal music, first the melodic mould is set by singing vocables, and then the song text is superimposed on it. Moreover, the elaboration of a melody leads to the corresponding elaboration in the text.

Santali language itself is modified when it is used in music. The four 'checked' consonants – K, C, T and P – of the Santal language used at the end of words are not pronounced while singing. Also, it is noticed that sometimes words that begin with vowels are prefixed with 'n' when used in music.[3]

It should be noted here that the Santal membranophones are all fixed pitch instruments. At the final stage of making, the makers do the tuning of these instruments depending on their feel of the pitch of the songs. Unlike in other music traditions, these instruments are not tuned according to the basic note of the singer; it is the singer who follows the pitch of the instrument. Herein lies the intimate bond between Santal music and Santal musical instruments. Invariably, before a song begins, a short piece is played on *Tumdaks* and the singers start their song according to the pitch of these instruments.

## THE NATURAL AND SOCIAL CONTEXT

The song and dance of different genres as well as musical instruments of the Santal are connected to their various *Paravs* (festivals) and rituals. However, as Choksi has pointed out, "other genres such as *Lagre*, are specified by their ability to be performed at any time or place."[4] The point to remember here is that natural and social contexts are constitutive of these festivals – such as the harvest festival, the hunting festival, the festival for the gathering of medicinal plants, the flower festival, occasions for recitation of ancestors' stories – and so on. Thus, for instance, in *Sakhrat*, the hunting festival of the Santals, the *Tamaks* and *Tirios* are used during the trips to the forest. The *Tamak* is primarily associated with the hunting events of the Santals.

A Santal story says: "[o]nce upon a time a leopard in a forest started eating the cattle of the Santal residing in the neighbouring villages. The Santal decided to hunt and kill the leopard. On the day of the hunt, the people brought along many drums [*Tamakko*] and started drumming. You cannot imagine the din ... it felt as if the ground was turning upside down. The leopard took fright and ran away."[5] Clearly, the *Tamak* is used for making noise and for signalling, also sometimes used in dances. It is a hunting and war drum.

During *Dasae*, it was essential to play the *Huki*. When villagers went to the forest they sometimes came face to face with a tiger. In order to please the spirit of the tiger (*Baghut Bonga*), the roar of tiger is imitated through *Huki*. Santal musical instruments are deeply embedded in traditional practice.

## MANAGEMENT OF MUSICAL KNOWLEDGE

Santal music follows the system, generation, transmission, retention and retrieval of musical knowledge, through an ancient oral-aural and participative method. Memory and traditions are its two basic elements. It will not be wrong to say that despite the development of a considerable literate tradition over years, the Santal retained a mind-set of oral learning in this particular domain, not unlike Indian classical music. In the oral-aural tradition, knowledge remains inherent in the person of the knower. Knowledge and the knower here

1

2

3

4

5

6

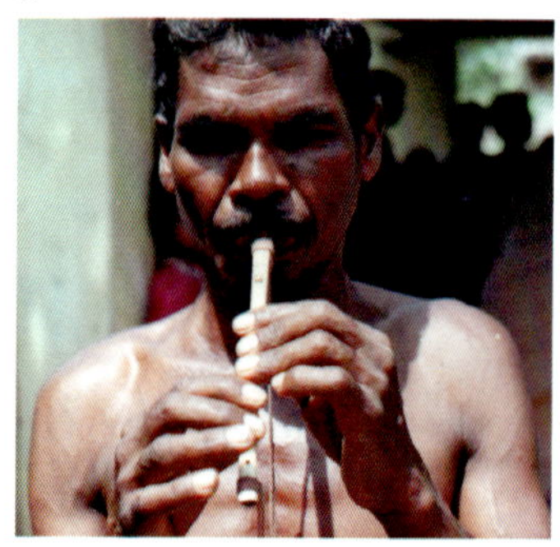

7

8

9

1. *TAMAK (NAGRA)*
A cup-shaped single-headed kettledrum made with an iron shell and buffalo skin. *Tamak* is made in two sizes: the smaller one, with an approximate diameter of 35 cm is played along with a *Tumdak*, while the larger one, with an approximate diameter of 41 cm accompanies *Borho Dhols. Tamaks*, worn around the neck using a leather strap, are played with two sticks, around 21 cm long.

2. *TUMDAK (MADAL)*
A hand-struck two-headed cylindrical drum made of burnt clay shells with buffalo skin, cowhide or goatskin. *Tumdaks* are always made in pairs and tuned together in the same pitch. The left side produces a deeper sound than the right one. The *Tumdak* is worn around the shoulders with a *Kandhach* (leather strap), and played with the hands.

3. *BORHO DHOL*
A two-headed cylindrical drum made from the wood of Mango, Jackfruit or Goomar Teak trees. *Borho Dhols* are made in pairs. Two types of skins are used to make its *Chhauni* (mouth cover): goatskin for the left mouth and cowhide for the right. The *Borho Dhol* is worn around the shoulders with a *Kandhach* (leather strap). The left side is played by hand, while the right side is struck using a curved stick.

4. *HUKI*
A cylindrical instrument made from the thick branches of hardwood trees such as Mango. Unlike other membranophones of the Santals, the *Chhauni* (mouth cover) of the *Huki*, positioned in front of the performer, is cut away so that the right fist can be put smoothly into the body of the instrument. Through a small incision at the centre of the other *Chhauni*, the shaft of a peacock feather is inserted and knotted from the outside. The performer pulls the entire length of the shaft through the instrument to produce a deep muffled sound. The *Huki* is almost extinct.

5. *TIRIO*
A large side-blown bamboo flute, without a beak but with a special blowhole. It is made of a type of bamboo called *Muli*. The piece of bamboo that is used for making this instrument must have two nodes. It has seven holes – one mouth hole for blowing, and six finger holes. Air strikes the inside walls near the two nodes at the two ends of the bamboo and the sound is produced as it starts vibrating inside the *Tirio*. Manipulating the air passage on the six finger holes produces notes. *Tirios* are made in pairs.

6. *BANSHI*
A 'beaked flute' that is held vertically. Air is blown into the flute through a beak. Controlling this airflow through the finger holes produces different notes. Finger holes may vary in number from four to eight.

7. *MAURALI*
A flute made from the wing-bone of a vulture, it is about 18 to 21 cm in length with a square hole at one end of the bone. It is held vertically and has no beak. There are six finger holes. Though it looks like a mouth hole, air is not blown through the square opening but through the hollow end on top of this hole. A small square piece of wood is pushed through this hole to partially block the opening. Sound is produced when air is blown through the open end of the *Maurali* and strikes the edge of the wood. The instrument is now extinct.

8–9. *BANAM*
A stringed instrument, a bowed monochord, and the only Santal instrument to be categorized as a chordophone. It is carved out of a single piece of soft wood and the *Chhauni* or skin cover is made from animal skin. This skin cover (*Banam Maurali Chhauni*) is usually made of goatskin. Earlier, the skin of a type of monitor lizard, *Gosaap* was also used. The playing string is tied with a peg fixed in a hole on the right side of one section.

The bow of the *Banam* is made from a thin piece of bamboo or wood, which is curved to the right shape. A traditional *Banam* is played with the bow held in the right hand. The notes are produced by lightly pressing the index and middle fingers of the left hand on the string or *Sadom* (made of silk thread). The *Banam* follows the melodic structures of songs. *Banams* that have figures carved into the wood, usually heads of *Pilchu Haram* and *Pilchu Budhi*, are called *Kindri Banam*.

The larger *Banam* is the *Dhodro Banam*. There is also the *Huka Banam* or *Reta Banam*, made from coconut shell and bamboo. The bow is traditionally made from bamboo strip and *Sisal* fibre curved to the right shape. A similar instrument is *Phet* or *Pheton Banam*, a plucked rather than bowed monochord. It has a finger board and one guitar peg fixed at top for tying the thread.
It is plucked by a tiny piece of the pointed end of a cow's horn. The name, *Phet Banam*, may have some connection with the system of playing this instrument. The word *Phet* in Santali means: let go anything pulled tight or play on a string.

are one and indivisible. Hence, knowledge is transmitted and learnt, retained and retrieved, from generation to generation, through social and cultural exchange within the community, on the occasion of festivals, rituals and rites of passage. Skills are acquired through apprenticeship/discipleship, by listening and repeating, by assimilating formulary materials and, by participation in a kind of corporate retrospection – not by abstracted and individualized study in the strict sense.[6] However, radical changes in historical circumstances and interactions between Santals and mainstream sections of our society through state-sponsored development programmes as well as various cultural activities over the years have created great complexities in every domain of Santal life. It is natural that at this juncture their music tradition should be in flux. Needless to say, changes are quicker and more unregulated in musical traditions that are based on psychodynamics of orality than in those based on literate traditions. As the latter is inscribed on outer surfaces, it takes longer to change.

At present, the music tradition of the Santals is facing different challenges arising out of (a) displacement from the original context (b) intervention in the conceptual location, (c) extinction of indigenous instruments, and, (d) changes imposed from outside – either for extra-musical considerations or for artificially bringing in a standardisation of musical tradition to suit the musical tastes or norms of the intervener, or both. We shall have a brief look at these four interrelated aspects and try to understand what poses the real threat to the tradition. I shall then place this tradition in a comparative framework, with another major oral-aural musical tradition of India, Indian 'Classical' Music, to see why and how the latter, despite facing similar challenges, has managed to preserve its distinctive traits through time.

(a) Displacement from the Original Context

There is a long history of Santal migration from their original habitat to different parts of our country. The socio-cultural and political specificities of the new locales have influenced the original musico-artistic traditions which have had to interact with the local folk/regional culture, as well as confront and negotiate the urban, middle class culture of the new location, in this case of West Bengal.

(b) Intervention in the Conceptual Location

In the case of Santali music, musical knowledge that was earlier located primarily in the performing subject of an oral-aural context has been 'externalised'. This usually happens when a music/dance performance is captured through sound/video technology. That performance of a specific moment is frozen for later reference. But the impact of intervention in the conceptual domain of a music tradition is strongest when the unique intonation pattern, which undulates and traverses between notes and microtones, is 'externalized' on keyboard instruments based on specific pitch points, like harmoniums or synthesizers. The fixing of notes on specific pitch points intervenes in its core area and leads to the gradual change of that music. 'Externalization' of song texts in written form or even the notated version of them act as a memory aid, and cannot but radically affect the musical thinking of a community.

(c) Extinction of Indigenous Instruments

Santali musical instruments are mostly made out of natural products, such as wood and animal skin. In the past, these materials were obtained by the Santal from the forest. Today there are forest laws, so these products have now to be purchased from the market, which makes them expensive and often beyond reach of the tribals. As a result, musical instruments like *Huki Banam, Borho Dhol* and *Tirio* that are made out of wood and bamboo are gradually becoming rare. The vulture, which was a very common bird in the focus area, is now a rare sight. So *Mauralis*, which are made from the wing-bone of vultures, are totally extinct. The *Tumdak* and the *Tamak* are faring better. The reason for this is that the makers have started using alternative materials such as burnt clay and iron shell, as well as the skin of domestic animals like cow, buffalo or goat, instead of wood and the skin of wild animals. It may be that the invention of the *Phet Banam* is a step in this direction. But in such experiments, care needs to be taken to maintain as much of the original timbre of the instruments as possible.

There are several consequences of the gradual disappearance of instruments. The sharp decline in their production leads to the gradual erosion of related knowledge and skills that had been preserved and transmitted over generations through the actual process of making the instruments. The instruments are bought and sold, often at high prices, by those not belonging to the Santal community. These instruments have a deeply significant symbolic value for the community, in the context of various festivals, rituals, rites of passage and so on. They are an essential aspect of the socio-cultural identity of the Santal. Instruments that are musically incompatible, if not antagonistic, to the Santal music tradition, are filling the void caused by their disappearance. Instruments like *Dafli, Maracus, Harmonium, Banjo, Tabla-Bayan, Tasa,* various drums and synthesizers, are being distributed as part of the programmes being organised by state and other agencies.

(d) Changes Imposed from Outside

There are several key ways in which change is being introduced. To begin with, there is the detrimental effect of the harmonium. In Santal musical culture, the *Tumdak* plays a very important role in determining the pitch of the song. Songs always begin after the *Tumdak* players play some short pieces. The pitch of the *Tumdak* thus sets the pitch that the singers follow. Even when *Tumdaks* are made, their tuning is done by the makers depending purely on their feel and experience of the pitch of Santal songs. The only exception is during solo singing with self-accompaniment of the *Banam* when the tension of the thread is adjusted according to the 'scale' of the singer. Harmoniums are disastrous for the intonation of this music. Being a keyboard instrument, the harmonium binds musical notes to standard frequencies or pitch points. Its use in Santal music will gradually lead to the destruction of the finer nuances of the Santal intonation pattern. It will also displace notes from their original positions in the Santal musical scale. Moreover, the use of the harmonium will transform the musical movement of these people from a gradual undulation or traverse across the finer intervals between two notes to a sharp leap from one note to another, destroying the very distinctiveness of Santal music of this area. Again, in itself, this inscribes the musical elaboration onto the keyboard and thus, in a way, externalizes the musical notes on an outer surface and distances this specific knowledge from the knower.

Music competitions are frequently organised at many levels, from village to state level. They cause a dissonance in the tribal cultural ethos in which the entire community participates in the music and dance festivals, where there is no distinction between performers and audience or viewers; hence there is no question of judging good or bad performance. Music competitions pitch one group of a community against another, radically changing the inclusive nature of the tradition into a competitive one. Also, those invited to give their judgement bring their own aesthetic yardstick, which is naturally quite distinct from the musical aesthetics of the Santal.

During these official events, the traditional spatial configuration of the performers is also changed. In their group dances Santal women typically form a semi-circle by holding each other's hands or waists while men play their musical instruments facing the dancers. But in experimental dances, women stand in a row (or two), one behind the other, in front of the microphones placed on the stage. Instrument players are placed behind the wings.

## CHANGE IN LANGUAGE OF SANTAL SONGS

It is common practice on the part of the local administration of this region to spread awareness of varous socially relevant issues — like literacy, family planning etc. — through songs composed in the Bengali language and set to melodic moulds of different songs of the Santal. Given the interconnection between Santali language and Santali song or the close text-tune relationship in Santal music, it can hardly be overstressed that change in language leads, logically and inevitably, to a distortion in the formal structure of different genres of Santal song. And the distortion of the formal structures of Santal songs changes the styles of their singing, dancing as well as that of instrumental accompaniment that closely follows the melodic and metric moulds of Santali songs.

## SANTAL VERSUS CLASSICAL MUSIC TRADITIONS

It is useful here to make the comparison between Santal and Indian classical music. Both are basically oral-aural traditions. But Indian classical music has been able to survive as a living tradition, maintaining its basic oral-aural traits within a literate, urban and 'high-technology' ambience. Its history reveals that, like the Santal musical tradition, it also faced challenges arising out of displacement from its original physical location and performance contexts. Indeed, it was shifted from temples to royal courts to rich men's parlours to modern-day impersonal concert halls in the big metropolises of India and abroad. Yet it survived and retained continuity in its three basic musical cornerstones — melodic structure (*raga*), rhythmic structure (*tala*) and song text (*prabandha*). The instruments of classical music kept alive their distinctive features, even while becoming progressively more sophisticated, both structurally and musically, over the years.

Such musical transformation became possible in the domain of classical music because of an extra-musical reason. As its history shows, the political exigencies of nineteenth-century India invested our *raga sangeet* with the epithet 'classical'. Whether or not this elevated the status of this music in the eyes of our colonial rulers is a different question, but the epithet certainly proved beneficial to the tradition. Its special status as the 'classical' music of India insulated it against mindless interventions in its core areas. Even today, there are attempts to reactivate the age-old institutions of *gharana*, which are specific musical styles developed around the male members of the family of a master musician. In its transmission and performance, memory and tradition still remain the basic foundation. Written 'texts' or scores are consciously and carefully avoided, though there is a formidable corpus of written and notated song texts. Moreover, in terms of patronage, this music has always enjoyed the favour of those in positions of power; in fact social prestige has always been associated with patronizing this music. In contrast, the community based music of peoples like the Santal does not enjoy such status or patronage.

The question then is about the strategies that we might borrow from classical music in order to bolster Santal music. The example of harmoniums is instructive here. Harmoniums were introduced into Indian classical music after considerable debate about its possible negative impact on the intonation pattern of Indian music. Indian 'classical' music faced the challenge of a keyboard instrument by changing the tuning system of this instrument from the system of tuning each note independently with the help of tuning forks to the system of tuning its notes on the basis of a consonance relationship. Nowadays harmoniums are tuned by following consonant relations between 1st–4th and 1st–5th notes (that is, on the basis of Sa–Ma and Sa–Pa (*Samvaditva* or consonance), depending on the tuner's feel of such relationship. Also, classical music soon began to cleverly use both types of intonations without one having to replace the other: (1) the undulating one through the extensive use of appropriate embellishments during the slow movement, and, (2) fixed pitch points when fast tempo is required. If anyone carefully observes the system of accompaniment provided by expert harmonium players when the musical movement is slow, it will be seen clearly that the harmonium is used to fill the gaps when the musician takes a short pause and to provide steady notes on consonance points in which this instrument has already been tuned. But at fast speed when *taans* (an ornamentation in fast speed) or similar ornamentations are used, the instrument follows each note of the singer and thus provides a real support to the musician for staying in specific pitch points. Unfortunately, no debate has emerged on the use of harmoniums in Santal music. The areas where the Santal live are simply being flooded with this instrument without careful thought as to its use and impact.

In the past, classical music was a combination of vocal and instrumental music as well as dance, and was referred to as just *sangeet*. This was similar to Santal music. Another aspect of the classical tradition is that each branch—vocal, instrumental and dance—developed over time as independent art forms. This trend of separation is also slowly developing now in the domain of Santal music. This becomes evident when we see *Banam* players calling themselves *Banamraja* or 'King of Banam', and performing solo pieces at Santal weddings and various other celebrations in return for a reasonable fee. Sometimes we also see on such occasions a group of young Santal men playing professionally on different kinds of drums along with synthesizers, casio, etc. It will be interesting to observe the long-term impact of this growing professionalism and the way it negotiates modern technology and the market. Innumerable websites are already evidence of such trends. It may be that eventually these will create a space conducive to the continuation of Santal music as an independent and context-free art form.

1 Bodding, *A Santal Dictionary*, Gyan Publishing House, New Delhi, 1999, (1932–1936), V. 4, p. 720 (under entry: phot). Also Bodding, *Santal Folk Tales*, Gyan Publishing House, New Delhi, 1997 (1925–1929), V. I, p. 216 (fn. 24). The word *phet* in the context of the story 'The Jackal and the Hare' is used "about a branch or the like striking when suddenly released from having been turned aside; it is also used about playing with fingers or a small bit of wood on a stringed instrument" [emphasis mine].

2 Choksi, 'Scripting Autonomy: Script, code and performance among Santali Speakers in Eastern India,' unpublished thesis, University of Michigan, 2014.

3 Prasad, 'Text-Tune and Tone-Tune Relations in Santal Music: Some Preliminary Observations,' pp. 235–241 in Bonnie Pvt C. Wade (Ed.) *Text, Tone And Tune: Parameters of Music in Multicultural Perspective*, Oxford & IBH Publishing Co. Ltd., New Delhi, 1993.

4 Choksi, *ibid.*

5 Bodding. P O, 'The Jackal and the Leopard' in *Santal Folk Tales*, Gyan Publishing House, New Delhi, 1997, V. 1, p. 11.

6 Choksi, *ibid.*

# SERENADING THE WORLD
## The Music of the Santals

Ludwig Pesch

The Santal people of India have made a considerable contribution to world culture. Many artistic pioneers of modern India have acknowledged the influence of the Santal. Rabindranath Tagore (1861–1941), who in 1913 became India's first Nobel laureate, lived with the Santals in Santiniketan at the turn of the century and wrote of the enduring impact of their culture. The young Bengali flautist Pannalal Ghosh (1911–1960) spent many months in the countryside with the Santals. He would go on to find fame as a film composer and classical flautist, but fondly recalled his friendship with the Santals and how they made music together, remembering that time as the happiest of his life.

Santal influence was felt not just in music but also in the visual arts — in the works of Jamini Roy, Nandalal Bose, Ramkinkar Baij — modern theatre and education. We may speak of an influence that reaches far beyond the Santal region, nourished by the fusion of many different disciplines. But it is a gentle and inconspicuous influence, a sort of 'whispered dialogue' in keeping with the persistence and modesty of the Santals themselves. Visiting a remote Santal village is bound to be a memorable experience. Subtle bonds also connect the Santals of Jharkhand and Bangladesh with the residents of Kolkata and Mumbai. In fact, contact increasingly extends to the global South Asian diaspora. For Rabindranath Tagore and many of his followers, the constant search for harmony with nature and for authenticity was and remains a meaningful pursuit.

### SANTAL INSTRUMENTS

The Santals form India's largest tribal community, numbering approximately six million. They are spread across several Indian states besides Bangladesh and Nepal. The majority of the Santals living in West Bengal and its neighbouring regions are agriculturists. At the same time they are highly regarded as talented musicians and dancers. Moreover, Santal women possess a self-assurance that puts the social norms of rural India into question, for they not only participate in cultural life, but also choose their own life partners.[1]

The Santals pride themselves on religious practices that are quite distinct from 'mainstream' Hinduism. Suffice to mention here that social, political and psychological pressures mark the urban culture of the Santals. This is particularly so in the state of Jharkhand, where they have long been sought to be converted by Hindus and Christians alike.[2]

In many of the world's industrialised regions, the musical instruments of indigenous communities become either museum pieces or symbols of emancipation. Santal musicians find themselves caught between competing forces — the ever-present Indian mass media and the interests of politicians. A shifting play of prestige and neglect determines the social status of many traditional musical instruments. This is particularly true of the stringed instruments that accompany Santal songs. They belong to the large family of *Sarangi* lutes. Depending on their workmanship and use, they are described either as *Banam* (*Dhodro Banam, Phet Banam*) or *Sarinda*. Unlike the *Sarangi* played by classical musicians, the instruments favoured by the Santals have very few strings. They are loved for their gentle sounds, an effect that is unfortunately lost on the modern stage. During Santal social occasions like weddings, several wind instruments are also used: a straight sort of trumpet (*Bair*) for processions, an S-shaped copper instrument (*Shinga*) and a small double-reeded instrument (*Shenai, Shahnai*). The latter plays an important role in various performances of the musical life of rural societies, both in the Indian subcontinent and beyond its borders.

Most Santal songs and dances pertain to particular seasons and life events. During the *Baha* flower festival in spring, it is common to invite all who are present to sing and dance along. Here the bamboo flute (*Tirio*) is indispensable. It complements instruments also to be found in other indigenous and classical traditions.[3]

During major festivals, iron kettledrums send out an unmistakeable invitation to the neighbouring communities. They then accompany what can sometimes be hundreds of participants. Depending on the region and event, the participants themselves play on drums made of wood or clay (*Madal, Madol, Mandal Tumda*), small gongs (*Bata*) and cymbals (*Kartal*). Anklets with brass bells (*Junko, Nupur*) emphasise the rhythm with their characteristic chime, which also rings through the Jhumur dances so popular amongst Bengalis.

### SONG TEXTS AND SINGING

An integral part of the musical heritage of the Santals is formulaic healing chants: the parts of the body are addressed one after the other, from head to toe. The repetition of each verse not only carries a symbolic meaning but also helps preserve an extremely important collective memory. In many tribes in Odisha, the singers invoke the god *Karam Devta* and the goddess *Karamasani*, just as the Santals do.

Children are sometimes integrated into social, economic and cultural life according to their skills. And just as in the realms of classical music, dance and in vernacular theatre, this begins with hearing and singing along with the chorus. After this, the children learn

*Junko or Nupur* (Anklets with brass bells), 2014

to set the beat with the help of hands and cymbals; later, they also take on organisational responsibilities.[4] Here authentic transmission takes priority over creativity and variations are limited to song lyrics. The traditional melodies of the Santals are internalised through the use of non-lexical Tahareta syllables.[5] A melody may thus be combined with appropriate lyrics to suit any particular occasion such as a wedding.

Santal music is part of a long history of shifting relationships between different ethnic and social communities in India. It would therefore be inappropriate to view the dwindling significance of any particular instrument as a symptom of an 'endangered' or indeed 'primitive' culture. The very opposite may indeed be true: encounters with Santal culture has left its mark in various aspects of Indian life. This is evident in the music of the rebellious poet-composer, activist and journalist, Kazi Nazrul Islam (1899–1976). Many of his popular songs (Nazrul Sangeet, Nazrul Geeti), composed for Kolkata's film industry, are based on a syncopated rhythm, which he borrowed from the *Jhumur* dance of the Santals. Unlike Tagore, he grew up in the countryside. Yet like Tagore, he was committed to women's rights, having seen that these had already been realised in Santal communities and other Indian tribes.[6]

The modest bamboo flute, with which Kazi Nazrul Islam is associated even today, crosses between personal and public spheres, between an inner and an outer world. Only a few decades earlier, its sound filled the straw-covered Santal villages that inspired so many of Tagore's poems and songs. He felt responsible both for the welfare of the Santals and for the preservation of their culture.

Those who take the time to explore the rural surroundings of the 'World University' (Visva Bharati) founded by Tagore in Santiniketan will understand why he felt alienated from the urban life of his birthplace, the imperial capital Kolkata. What is palpable here is the meaning of an ecological way of life. For the Santals, this is as worthy of preservation as their language and music. A Santal festival song emphasises the original point of music making as a part of everyday life:

*As the sounds of the flute fill up all my senses*
*Even the dead flowers in my hair knot blossom anew.*[7]

1 See Klein, 2006, p. 77: "There is no woman (of the Santals) who cannot dance or sing, and no man, who doesn't beat the drum or play the flute [...]. Along with the zest for life, feeling of community, modern understanding of democracy and special status of women, the children, too, enjoy many freedoms."

2 Santal converts, or their descendants, are increasingly pushed by a coalition of political parties to declare themselves members of the so-called Sarna natural religion and ancestor worship or, if need be, to convert back to it. The modern Sarna movement understands itself as a branch of Hindu nationalism that challenges the secular character of the Indian constitution and also the right to (self-) conversion (See Hembrom, 2013 and others).

3 Anthropologists are convinced that the Santals never lived in total isolation from neighbouring societies. In the light of changing modes of employment in urban regions (especially in the state of Jharkhand), generalisations including the concept of 'connectedness to nature' should be treated with caution.

4 The music ethnologist Ashok Ranade (1999) emphasises that the high status of non-written transmissions connects very different ethnic groups and social layers in India. This pertains equally to recitations from the Rigveda and to the rituals of indigenous tribes.

5 Videoclips and background information on this widespread method is available to those interested on http://sam.mimemo.net/. These were produced in Kerala in conjunction with a research project at the Bern University of Arts under the title 'Sam, Reflection, Gathering Together! Voices and hands in traditional Indian (dance) theatre'.

6 Kazi Nazrul Islam remains popular among Bengali Hindus, Muslims and Santals of all age groups, even decades after Independence. Within his lifetime he was recognised as the national poet of Bangladesh, which achieved its independence from Pakistan in 1971.

7 Kämpchen, 2000, p. 5.

# PLAYING WITH PERSPECTIVES
## The Santal *Baha* Festival
Marine Carrin

Santal music is integral to their religion, which in turn is deeply interwoven with nature – the forest, the cycle of seasons and the hunting-gathering traditions of a tribal community. One of their prominent festivals is called the *Baha Bonga*, which means, literally, flower (*Baha*) and god or ancestral spirit (*Bonga*). *Baha Bonga* is celebrated in early April, when the *mohua* flowers[1] and the *sal*[2] buds are blooming. The festival takes place in the *Jaher* (sacred grove) which shelters the stones dedicated to the *Bongas* of the creation myth: *Marang Buru*, his wife *Jaher Era* and their sons, the five brothers called the *Monreko* who have a common wife of Hindu origin, *Gosaen Era*. The festival lasts two days during which men and women sing and dance in the sacred grove at different moments of the ritual, to the accompaniment of traditional musical instruments.

Though the Santal do not explicitly link flowers with ancestors they compare the renewal of nature with human reproduction, symbolized by the double metaphor of flower and bone – the flower standing for the uterus and the bone for the lineage.[3] As part of the funeral rites, after cremation, the mourners decorate the bones of the deceased's neck and head with *golanchi* flowers. The son of the deceased pours milk and rice beer on the 'flower bones' to regenerate them. Similarly, a girl says that she is blooming (*Baha Kanai*) when she is menstruating and cannot cook for the family. Even today, nobody would dare to pluck wild fruits and flowers before the *Baha* festival, fearing the ancestors' wrath. If a man transgresses this taboo, his ancestors will be polluted and bring disease not just on their descendants but also on other clans.

### THE RITUALS OF *BAHA BONGA*

The village priest, the *Naeke*, and his wife, the *Naeke Era*, as well as those who will dance in the sacred grove must stay chaste on the eve of the festival. On the first day, the village priest erects a shelter made of *Sal* for the stones of the *Jaher Bongas*, the deities of the grove. The village homes and the sacred grove are purified with cow dung.

When it is dark, the village headman offers the *Naeke* a new *dhoti* as well as a *sari* for his wife from the community. The elders of the different village clans come to the *Naeke's* house, with three chicken and are followed by three young men[4] who show signs that they are possessed (*Rumok'*) by the *Bongas*. The priest sprinkles their face with water, adorns them with white cloths and respectfully salutes them, recognizing them as the deities of the sacred grove and as the oracles of *Baha*.

The next day, everyone goes to the *Jaher* where the priest and his wife receive the emblems of the deities who will possess the boys: three winnowing vans, a necklace, and wristlets, a set of bow and arrows, and a pot of water. The *Naeke* solemnly puts the necklace and wristlets in a basket and covers it with the bow and arrows and his own sacrificial knife; the knife, too, will become an emblem of the *Jaher* deities. Finally, the *Naeke Era* places the pot of water on the ancestor altar of her husband. Later, they will read the oracle of the hunt at the surface of the water. The villagers sing a prayer (*bhakhen*) in homage to *Jaher Era*, the guardian of the sacred grove:

*We salute you, Mother Jaher Era*
*On the occasion of the Baha festival,*
*we offer you*
*Young fowl, new flowers, freshly husked rice*
*We beg you to accept it with love*
*We have taken these new flowers and fruit*
*Let there be no disease and no sickness*
*When we are out in the forest hunting*
*Make the animals appear before us*
*When our animals, goats and cows are grazing,*
*Let the tigers leave them alone,*
*Let no disease enter the village*
*Bring the rain-bearing clouds in time*
*and let the earth be fresh and green*
*Bless everything with new life*

The villagers start to sing and dance. The songs (*seren*) should help the *Bongas* enter the body of the possessed boys. Unlike the prayer, the songs do not follow a linear narrative but weave different mythic themes around the idea of the ancestors as hunters and gatherers. *Mohua* flowers are the first to be plucked but other flowers are gathered by the women and represent additional food.

The songs integrate spirit and matter, corporal reality and heroic dimensions of the ancestors, to fashion a world where the boundaries between the participants and their environment become permeable. Ritual thus becomes an experience of playing with perspectives since ritual allows mimesis – the human faculty to "yield into and become Other."

### MYTH, SONG AND RITUAL

During the *Baha* festival, the songs evoke different themes non-sequentially, which echo many of the themes of the ritual. While the villagers dance in the sacred grove, the oracles merge with the mythic fathers and return to the sacred places of the Santal. The songs recreate a time when the village, or the women, waited for the hunters to return with food, or from the clan wars. The song makes the mimesis come true, and when the oracles return, they are the mythic hunters the women have waited for. To act as hunters the oracles take bows and arrows and they return with the precious *mohua* flowers.

The forest becomes the main theme of the songs and it is a resounding forest. The hunters are blowing the horn but so do the deities, echoing the songs of the villagers. This sound is not just music, it alludes to a mythic disorder compared to epilepsy, a metaphor used to describe the "wars between the clans."
The poetic parallelism compares the villagers waiting for the oracles with the ancestors lingering in the primordial forests. The visual imagery of the songs gradually becomes peaceful; women adorn their waits, since men are driving epilepsy away. The songs allow the singers, and especially the women, to partially change their perspective of the world to relate to that of the hunters but also of non-humans, deities and animals. The metaphors of the songs help identify the oracles and the men as ancestors who used to gather and hunt in the mythic forests.

The songs then describe how the hunters find overflowing rivers, and a mysterious black flower which evokes the errors of the ancestors while a white flower stands as a metaphor for knowledge—an allusion to the *ojha's* (priest) disciples who explore the cosmos to find knowledge in the sky, allowing them to get possessed and address the deities during the rituals of healing. For the women, the return of the oracles is compared to the return of the hunters. The forest, which provides flowers, fruits, tubers and game, becomes the place where one encounters war and death. The blowing of the horn marks the wars, but when the fight ceases, the village horn sounds to announce the return of the oracles and the celebration of the festival.
When the oracles return with a basket full of *mohua* flowers they enter into trance, shaking their shoulders and jerking violently, and moving their head from left to right with eyes closed. In the songs, possession is described as disorder since the oracles are chosen by the deities and do not control their trances. During possession, human and spirit realities obviously fuse, as Stoller suggests.[5] This knowledge is embodied when the oracles wear the paraphernalia of the *Jaher* deities, the necklace and the wristlet that are evoked in the songs and connected with mythical time.

While in the songs, the hunters fetch a black flower and later the flower of knowledge itself, the oracles bring back the *mohua* flowers which are symbols of fertility. After questioning the oracles, the priest sprinkles the flowers with sacred water and gives one *mohua* flower to each woman of the village.
Then the villagers sprinkle each other with the fertility water that comes from the *mohua* flowers. The anxiety expressed in the songs when waiting for the oracles is appeased and villagers dance and rejoice. The songs help us to grasp the emotional link that unites the oracles to the *mohua* flowers, since the possession *rumok* makes them like the flowers that contain the essence of possession.

THE SONGS: *BAHA SEREN*
A girl, Chita, is addressed by a voice, presumed to be *Jaher Era*, the guardian of the sacred grove. The voice questions Chita, who does not always answer.
The verses evoke mythic times, situations that contrast with events in the sacred grove, where villagers are waiting for the return of the oracles. The songs invite the participants to cross over ontological boundaries and experience the waiting as another mode of knowing. Every animal, plant or character is personified in the songs, to allow the singers to take their point of view.

*What are you waiting for Chita,*
*you who are staying behind?*
*What are you waiting for, O Gosaen?*
*My fathers have gone for hunting*
*Is this the reason for your waiting?*
*Waiting for them it is getting late*
*While the men are delayed I am combing my hair*
*I apply khol and unguent to my eyes when they are late*
*With a deep sound, child hare*
*In the darkness, child leopard, they are coming*
*With a deep sound the child hare and the child leopard*
*are crying* (repeated)

[Chita seems to wait for her fathers, her paternal kin, also the ancestors and the hunters. The young woman imagines the "fathers" as she is "seeing" them, a metaphor alluding to the wife of the hunt priest (*Dihuri Era*) who watches the progress of the hunters from the water omen (*sagun kanda*). If the water turns red, like blood, game is abundant. Girls should not comb their hair during the hunt, since this may prevent the hunters from finding their way back to the village. But since her kin are late, the girl does not care, though she hears the "deep sound" of hare and leopard roaming near the village. The frequent reference implies that the hunters have killed hares and leopards.]

*On the burnt hill, in Ghantabari, they were hunting,*
*they were in crowd*
*My fathers went towards the uncultivated fields*
*O Gosaen! they went towards the Sin forest*
*O Gosaen! they went towards the Man forest,*
*While hunting they found a black flower*
*O Gosaen! while hunting we see the buds opening*

Santal celebration, November 2014

[Women sing of how the hunters left the burnt hills of Ghantabari to hunt in an uncultivated field. Women then change perspective to remind the audience of what happened in Ghantabari. Women are not expected to talk about hunting in public, so through the song they reveal what they usually conceal, that they know the myth as also about the quarrel between the clans, a matter for men where they did not take part. The burnt hill alludes to shifting cultivation and the uncultivated field in the dispute, when some clans went to the Sin forest and others to the Man.]

*Chita, it seems that I shall adorn*
*myself with flowers*
*O my father your bow and arrow*
*On the burnt hill, there is the silkworm*
*In Ghantabari they are fighting*
*Why are you roaming*
*Why with lassitude*
*O Father! are you roaming like a betrothed boy?*
*With your bow you are roaming aimlessly.*

[The girl has adorned herself as women do for the *Baha* festival, which celebrates the grace of the girls who will blossom like flowers and then become mothers. The father, the hunter who carries his bow and arrow and is likened to the silkworm – a metaphor evoking the ancestors, likening them to silkworms in their cocoons before they settled in villages. The 'father' is then compared to a betrothed youth, an enigmatic image alluding to marriage and fertility that impregnates the *Baha* festival. The father as betrothed boy seems lost as if hesitant to get married, probably since marriage and sedentary village life are less appealing than roaming in the forest.]

*Ah Gosaen! there is a dead child!*
*Twice dead he is*
*Do not hunt him, Gosaen!*
*He is thirsty for water, Gosaen*
*There is the child hare*

[The girl laments to Gosaen of the death of a hare, portrayed as a child. Hares, in folk-tales, are seen as the double of human beings. The hare is twice dead, since humans should not kill this friendly animal.]
*We fondled the young dog*
*We clutched the falcon*

*It is said that I shall bring the chest of the partridge*
*It is said that I shall bring the hindquarter of the hare*
*The hunters have gone beyond the river*
*The hunters have thrown a profusion of arrows*

[The "we", here, refers both to girls and hunters as if the girls, while imagining the hunt, were themselves becoming hunters. The feeling of closeness to the animal world is expressed in hunting narratives[6] where hunters stress they should spare young animals to allow the game to reproduce, or when they explain to the game that they must kill in order to survive, a point stressed by Ingold.[7] The hunters have just shared some game and bring the rest back to the village. Now the hunting becomes more intense, as the hunters cross a river and throw a "profusion of arrows" before getting out of breath.]

*My brothers have staggered,*
*O Gosaen! give them breath*
*The forest is sounding,*
*The village horn is sounding*
*Who makes the forest resound so strongly?*
*In the village, another horn is sounding*
*The five have met*
*The six have adorned their waist*
*The five make the forest sounds*
*The village horn is sounding*
*Jaher Era is blowing the horn*

[Here, the song becomes more dramatic, as if the hunters were not sure to return. Suddenly, "the forest is sounding." Probably musical instruments such as flute or drums are sounding, but the song only mentions the horn.[8] In the sacred grove, the women ask *Gosaen* to give breath to the hunters. Not just the men, but 'the five', which are the sons of *Marang Buru* and of *Jaher Era*, are also blowing the horn. The deities make the forest sound, for music marks the renewal of Nature.]

*It is said that my fathers are driving away epilepsy*
*They awake medicinal plants to cure epilepsy*
*My brothers are hunting epilepsy with*
*the copper horn which is sounding*
*Ah Gosaen, my elder sister,*
*The Ganga is rising*
*While the river Sora overflows*

[A mythic disorder compared to epilepsy, is the metaphor used to describe the wars between the clans. Curiously, the word for epilepsy is mirgi which means a deer, since the epileptics are jumping like deer. Here the fathers try to cure epilepsy, using medicinal plants as if they were *Ojha* (priest) healers. The ancestors are blowing the horn and the sound of the dispute is so powerful that it causes the rivers to overflow.]

*The five brothers carry milk on their back*
*The six are six brothers and they are churning*
*milk with a regular movement*

[The five Santal brothers who, like the Pandavas[9] from the Mahabharata, have a common spouse, are churning milk, a process that also evokes creation in Hindu myth. The *mohua* flowers are white like milk, and the plucking of the flowers by the three oracles is compared to its churning, adding mythic resonance to a ritual that is renewed every year.]

*To whom belongs the cock?*
*To whom belong the village peacock?*
*To the five, O Jaher Era, belongs the cock,*
*To the five, the flower of sarjom, O elder sister!*

[The songs return to village life. Different domestic animals are mentioned, as the five brothers are no longer hunting anymore but keeping a cock, probably for sacrifice. They also keep the *sarjom* flower which stands for the ancestors and represent patrilineal descent. Finally, the elder sister is asked to distribute the *sarjom* flower to the five brothers. This is followed by a sharing of the game, while in the *Jaher* women wait impatiently for the return of the oracles, who appear carrying the *mohua* flowers and ornaments for the deities.]

*For the lady of the sacred grove,*
*this wristlet worn on the top of the arm,*
*this centipede*
*For Gosaen Era the nose ornament and the ring*
*For Marang Buru, a ring is hidden*
*inside the mohua flower*
*And this shows when he possesses men*
*For the village priest, elder sister, the sarjom flower*
*Two flowers are bought and paid for*
*in the village street*

[These ornaments are not just beautiful, but also have a time dimension. The bracelet of *Jaher Era* is a centipede, which symbolizes timelessness, since she is the eternal guardian of the sacred grove. The ring of *Marang Buru*, the creation god is made of *mohua* flowers and the priest explained that during the trances, the oracles feel this ring around their head as if they were *mohua* flowers themselves.]

*At Turi Pukuri, the cloth made of flowers*
*In the skirt made of flowers, Is found the milk flower*
*During seven days and seven nights*
*it has been raining fire,*
*Humans where have you been?*
*And you who are sleeping among thy companions!*
*You who adorned your waist!*

[The mythic journey continues to Turi Pokhori, and inside a cloth made of flowers, the ancestors found the milk flower called *Bidia Baha* or 'the Flower of Knowledge'. In *Dasae* songs, this flower symbolizes the *Ojha's* knowledge. This wisdom allows the singers to remember the fire rain when Thakur, the god of Hindu origin, tried to destroy the world created by *Marang Buru*, the Santal Creation god.[10] Thakur recreates the world by allowing a pair of wild geese to lay their eggs at the surface of the ocean. From these eggs two humans were born, a boy and a girl. The songs allude to this second creation of the world that is seen like a journey, the memory of which is lost. "Humans where have you been?" say the songs.]

*My fathers were hungry*
*My fathers were thirsty*
*Give me the sacrificial knife which is well-used*
*O foreigner who will be sacrificed?*
*If there is no sacrificial victim, O elder sister's husband you will take me*
*If the women are not present, the millet will not ripen*
*If the women are not present the paddy will not get red.*

[The hunger and thirst, once more, evoke the ancestors wandering in the mythic forests. The song turns to the sacrifice of fowl to the deities of the *Jaher*. But the sacrifice is compared to marriage and the bride stands metaphorically for the victim. The parallel is made explicit when the girl, pretending to address her elder sister's husband who arranges her marriage, compares herself to a sacrificial victim. The last lines are an allusion to women and fertility, which is a theme in the festival.]

## CONCLUSION

The metaphors in the *Baha Bonga* songs identify the oracles and the men as ancestors who used to gather and hunt in the mythic forests. The world of the songs is not merely human but consists of all creatures, deities and divine beings. The songs allow men and women to make the mimetic practice come true, since the plucking of the first flowers evokes the mythic gathering. The participants intuitively know that the songs refer to their past not as a structure but rather as a texture into which each element is woven, according to the different perspectives taken by the singers. This perspective change, as underlined by Viveiros de Castro, allows participants to decentralize themselves from their ordinary role, to assume a new relation to the world and themselves.

The songs express the value of possession, the essence of which has been hidden, in the *mohua* flower, by *Marang Buru* himself. As Taussig suggests, mimesis implies a "copying, or imitation and a palpable, sensuous, connection between the perceiver and the perceived". The songs convey through an iconic logic some truth that could be translated in words, "women are like flowers, they bloom and give fruits." When the priest distributes flowers to the women, he enacts this truth, shared by men and women, who then sprinkle each other with the *dak'baha* or 'fertility water'.

1 *Bassia latifolia, L.*
2 *Shorea robusta, L.*
3 Carrin-Bouez, 1986, Chap. 4.
4 They are not necessarily virgin but they fast and stay chaste on the eve of the ritual.
5 Stoller, 1995.
6 Moreover in folk-tales, animals are speaking like humans.
7 Ingold, 2000.
8 The horn *sakia* is made from the horn of a buffalo and is mainly used during the hunt.
9 The five Pandava brothers are married to the princess Draupadi, while the five Santal brothers have a wife who is from a lower caste.
10 The creation myths of the tribal groups are often stories of incest. Elwin (1949) described tribal cosmogonies where siblings create the world through an incestuous relationship. In the Santal myth, two siblings are enticed by *Marang Buru* to drink rice-beer. They forget they are brother and sister and make love. *Marang Buru* the tribal god considers that this is not too serious, but Thakur, a Hinduized god, feels it is high time to organize society and matrimonial prohibitions between kin. Cf. Carrin-Bouez and Bouez, 1976.

# PHOTOGRAPHS FROM 1988

Ravi Kant Dwivedi

Photographs of Santal puppetry taken by Ravi Kant Dwivedi (b. 1954) in 1988, in the Santal villages of Navasar (District Dumka, Jharkhand), Uttar Shiala, Dhanshara, Kashpukur, Benedanga, Kakash Nonedanga, (District Birbhum, West Bengal) and Baghmara (District Burdwan, West Bengal). These photographs are taken from the Ravi Kant Dwivedi private archives in New Delhi.

Ravi Kant Dwivedi is an artist, photographer and filmmaker based in New Delhi. He has documented rare practices and arts forms such as *Jadupatua* paintings, *Dhokra* metal craft, the *Gajon* ritual of Bengal, the mask dance of Rajbanshis, the rain-invoking rituals of North Bengal, the design of fishing traps and boats in the east coast of India, and tribal and folk puppetry of Eastern India, especially the *Chadar Badar* puppetry of the Santals.

# *CHADAR-BADAR* PUPPETRY



Ravi Kant Dwivedi

## INTRODUCTION[1]

*Chadar Badar* is a type of puppetry peculiar to the Santal. It is quite different from the string, rod, gloves and shadow puppetry that are popular elsewhere in India. The *Chadar Badar* is made of wood, bamboo and fabric, and works on a simple principle that is visible even in the string toys found in Harappan culture. The same principle applies for a rice pounding device used by Santals. *Chadar Badar* has a square fixed frame with canopy and a circular platform on which two rows of puppets are fixed facing each other. A hollow bamboo attached at bottom serves as stand. A string runs through this bamboo and ties all the puppets. When played, the circular platform can rotate and the head and hands of the puppets move up and down. A player performs the puppot show with a coordinated pull and push of his hand and leg. The show is accompanied by musicians who sing and dance. The *Chadar Badar* show depicts the actual dance performed by the Santals in their daily life.

*Chadar Badar* is popular among the Santals of Bihar and West Bengal. During the Bengali festival of *Durga Puja*, Santal puppeteers travel from village to village with their puppet stages and their musicians.

Four major field trips were undertaken in 1988 to gather the information on this craft and its purveyors. I travelled to selected areas of Santal Parganas, Birbhum, Burdwan, and Midnapore districts. In September, the Navasar puppeteers from Birbhum set up their puppets and performed for me informally. On my return during *Durga Puja* I concentrated on Birbhum district and the neighbouring area of Burdwan, spending ten days travelling with puppeteers, interviewing them and documenting their performance in written notes and photography. I also interviewed puppet makers, members of the audience, and village elders who remembered performances of the past.

## THE PUPPETEERS

Interestingly, the puppet maker, the owner and the puppeteer (performer) may be three different persons. Of the many puppeteers that I met, only Phechu Maddi and Hopna Hanshda had made their own sets, although Hopna's set had been out of use for about 10 years. Others had inherited or borrowed their sets or had them made by others. The puppeteers are all part-time carpenters, but they do not come from the same clan. They also do agricultural work either on their own land or for others. Bhulu Murmu and Hopna Hanshda have enough land, so do not need to perform for money. But most of the others appreciate the extra income.

While it takes some skill to make and set up the mechanism of the puppet stage, not much skill is required to operate it. The puppeteer must have a good sense of rhythm, however, and when the puppeteer sings as well, he needs also a keen sense of satire. The puppeteers usually perform for just four days, during Durga Puja — *Saptami* (seventh day) to *Dashami* (tenth day). Some puppeteers perform the year around, but this is rare. By and large, though they can use the extra income, puppeteers perform primarily because they like to, not because they need to.

## THE PUPPET AND THE STAGE

A complete set of *Chadar Badar* consists of 11 to 17 wooden puppets arranged in rows on the floor of a platform, below which is the mechanism for their manipulation. In most cases, only the top part of the puppet shows above the cloth that hides the mechanism. In only one case can the whole puppet be seen. Usually just the arms and sometimes the head moves; the legs also move in the example where the whole body is visible. Puppets can be made of any soft, smooth wood. They are carved with small chisels in simple fashion and then painted over with inoxpensive oil paint and dressed in cloth scraps, paper, foil, beads and feathers. The most common figures are familiar Santal types: groups of female dancers and of male drummers, figures of old men and women, and of jokers and birds. Phechu Maddi's set depicts scenes of Santal daily life, such as rice husking and winnowing.

The puppets are operated by means of a single cord attached to the puppets by a number of other cords. The puppeteer uses his foot to tug the chord to the beat of the drums; this moves the puppets' arms (and in one case, legs). At the same time, some puppeteers rotate the inner platform of the stage with a hand so that it turns before the audience. In other cases this platform is fixed. The stage is covered with two cloths: one is a sari that hides the mechanism and the puppeteer's hands. The other makes a canopy over the stage. Again Phechu Maddi's set is different and has no canopy. Together these make for a colourful and captivating performance, resembling the bioscopes (peep-shows) familiar in village *melas* (fairs) in north and east India.

## THE PERFORMANCE

During *Durga Puja* the Santals perform their annual *Danshai Puja* and dances. The mood in the villages is festive and people welcome the travelling performers and look forward to the entertainment.

The puppeteer's performance is accompanied by music and song. Drums, flutes and cymbals provide the music. A troupe may have as many as seven members; the most usual number is five. The troupe's arrival in the village is announced by the beating of drums. They cover 8–10 villages in a day.

The performers set up in front of individual houses, moving from house to house until everyone has had a chance to see the act. The audience varies from a handful to about twenty persons, and children tag along after the troupe and watch the performance many times. The villages may be Santal or Hindu, and even towns like Bolpur or Rampurhat are included. A single performance lasts from 5–15 minutes, depending on the receptivity of the audience. Money, paddy, rice, and dal are the main forms of payment. These are collected at the end of the performance in baskets brought along for the purpose.

Ram Hanshda of Baghmara village (Burdwan) gave a performance at three nearby villages on October 15, 1988. Ram had a full set of puppets, including the joker and the bird — a total of twenty figures. The songs were in Santali, which I asked him to translate into Bengali. The English version below is my own:

*The sun and moon rise over the horizon*
*When the sun sets, the moon rises,*
*The world lies in between.*
*The earth has four corners and three levels.*
*We love the earth — long may we live.*
*May our lives be happy.*

*We are foolish Santals*
*We understand nothing*
*We float beneath the plough in the water of the fields.*
*We drown.*
*The sons of gentlemen go to school.*
*They fly in planes.*
*We cannot progress because we are uneducated.*
*While going to wash clothes,*
*The daughter of a washer man drowns in the pond.*
*The boatman says, "Bring the net.*
*I am going to rescue her".*

*All our lives we are uneducated.*
*That's why we are stupid.*
*Look how stupid we are!*
*That's why we've lost our land.*

The making of a *Chadar Badar* does not seem to relate to any myth. Even the individual puppets, which vary to some extent from set to set, do not have any links to mythology. They are all everyday characters representing identifiable scenes. The songs sung with the show are simple songs usually sung in daily life and do not try to relate or describe the scene or characters of the show. In fact they are not even specially meant for the puppet shows. They are the usual Santali songs that one may hear (usually) women sing in small groups, arms linked, on their way back home after the day's work.

## CONSTRUCTION AND MECHANISM OF CHADAR BADAR SETS

The uniqueness of construction and mechanism of *Chadar Badar* puppets make it distinct from all other conventional puppet systems such as rod puppets, glove puppets or string puppets. One composite and portable set contains the stage, characters and props. It is manipulated by one person by simply tugging (or pulling) and releasing one string. *Chadar Badar* puppetry does not seem to be linked to any legend or myth. It is also extremely difficult to trace it back to a place of origin or beyond the recent past. The puppeteers state that they have "seen" performers with "*Chadar Badar*" sets coming from the "hills".

The name *Chadar Badar*, often also referred to as *Chadar Bandhani*, may be derived from the practice of *Bandhani* (tying) or covering a *Chadar* (cloth) around the lower part of the set. It is possible that a basic idea or mechanism thus picked up was later independently simplified or elaborated by individual makers into the object we now see. The basic principle involved in its construction is that of a *Dhenki* or husking paddle (which uses a lever and counterweight), and is very popular in rural Bengal, particularly among the Santals.

Since making of the frame of the puppet set could not be witnessed (commissions for new sets are rare) I could not photograph the parts in a knocked-down format. Neither was it possible to document the process at different stages. An attempt is made here to explain the mechanism with the help of sketches and photographs of a set belonging to Bhulu Murmu, which was one of the most complicated ones that I saw.
The total height including canopy is 198 cm. The width of the set is 70 cm. The whole set rests on a bamboo pole (*Shirapp*). The contraption does not have legs and is held erect by the performer. The main structure is divided into two parts, i.e., the base and the revolving stage (*Charkha*).

## THE BASE

Two pairs of wooden bars (A) and (B) (*Kumbhre and Dhera*) are fixed at right angles (SK-1) with a square hole (C) running through them. (A) and 'B' are fixed facing each other at a distance of about 20 cm with four bars 'D' (*Khunti*; SK-2). A strong bamboo pole (*Shirapp*) which has one end carved into a square (G) is inserted through 'C' of 'A' bars (SK-3).

The hole of the bamboo and that of (E) work as the bearing for the revolving stage. This base is solidly made with good hard timber (Jackfruit timber in this case) and even excluding the bamboo pole accounts for over

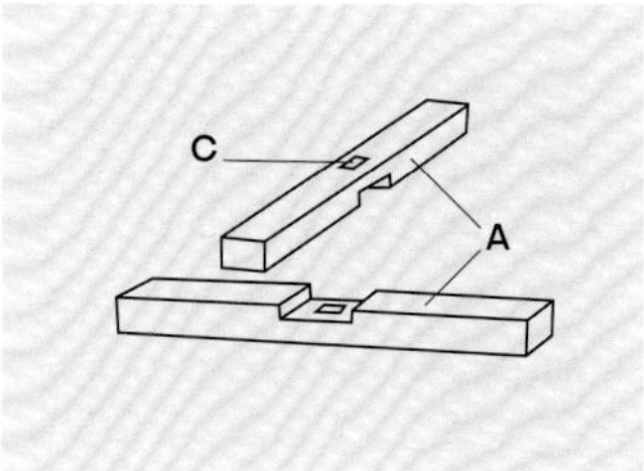

SK-1

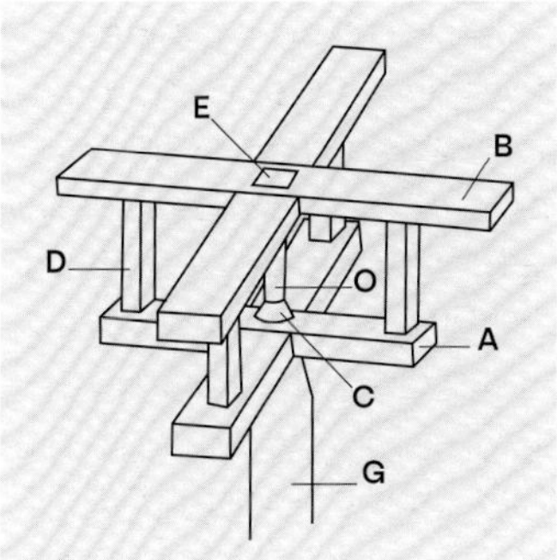

SK-2

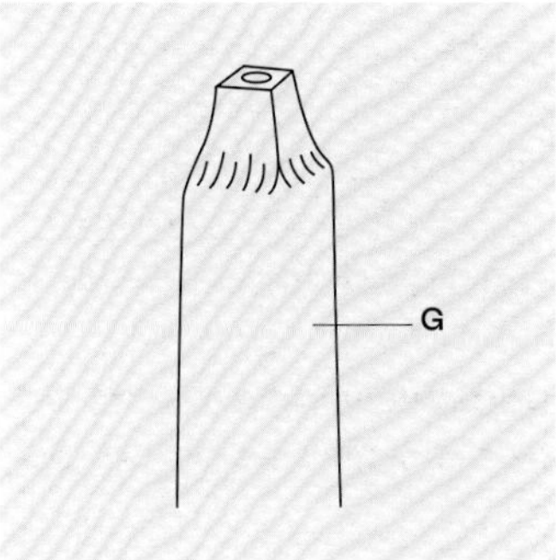

SK-3

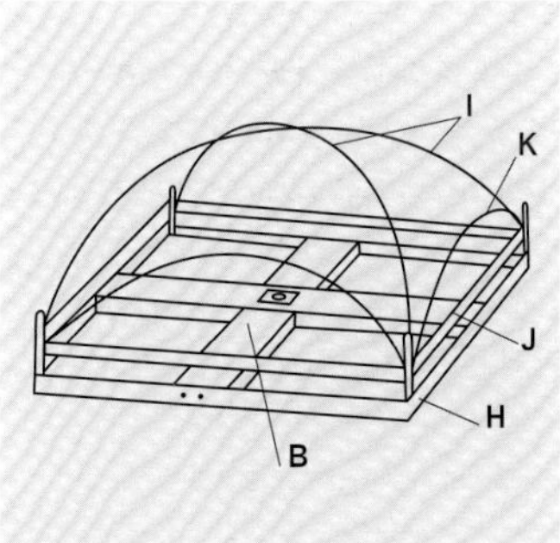

SK-4

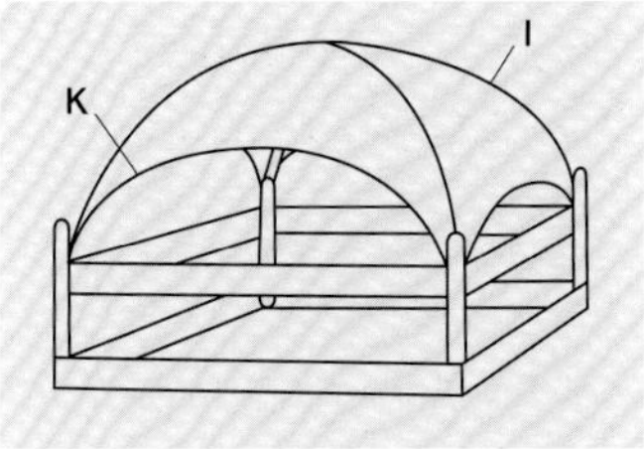

SK-5

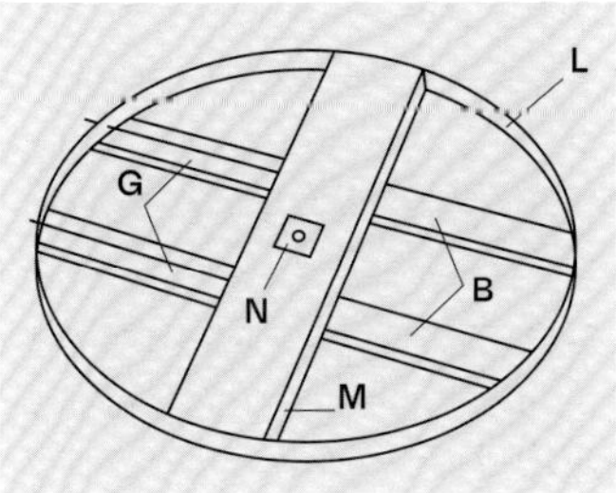

SK-6

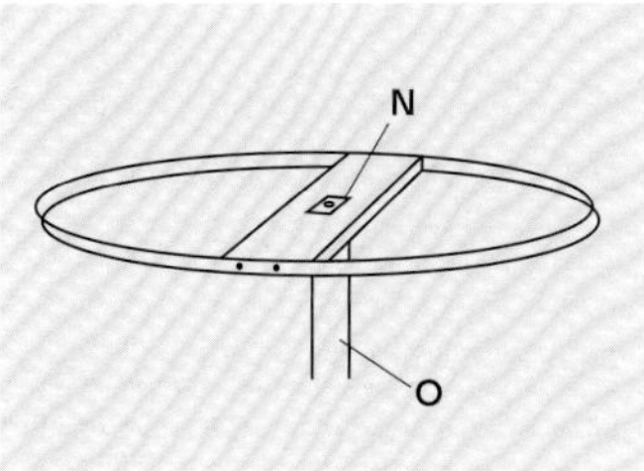

SK-7

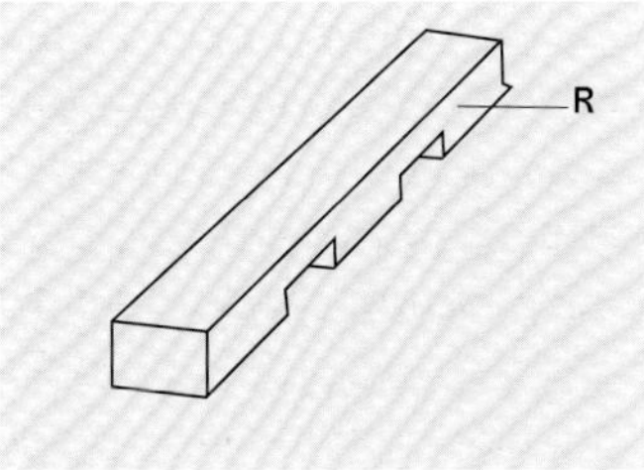

SK-8

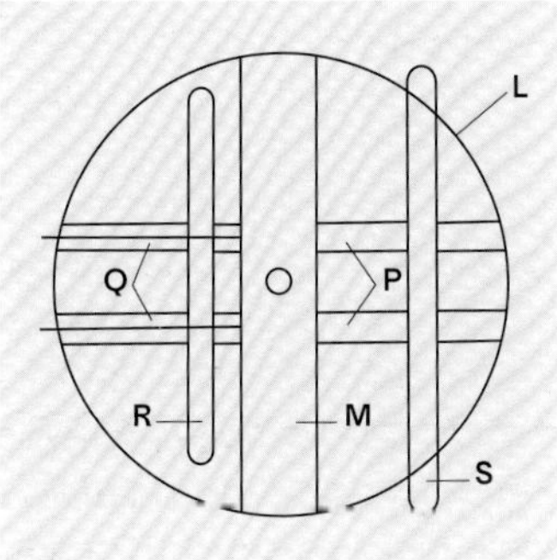

SK-9

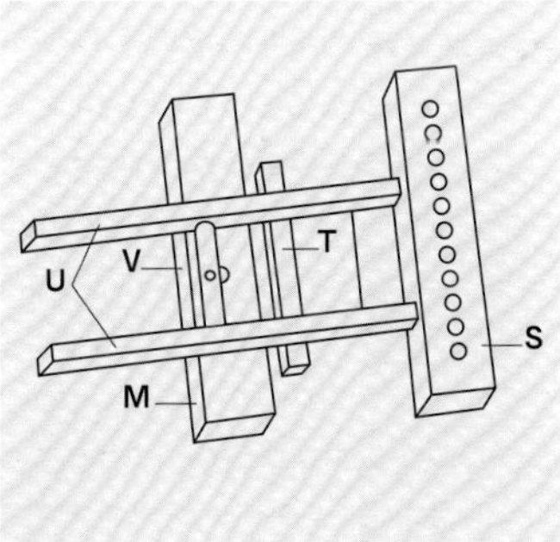

SK-10

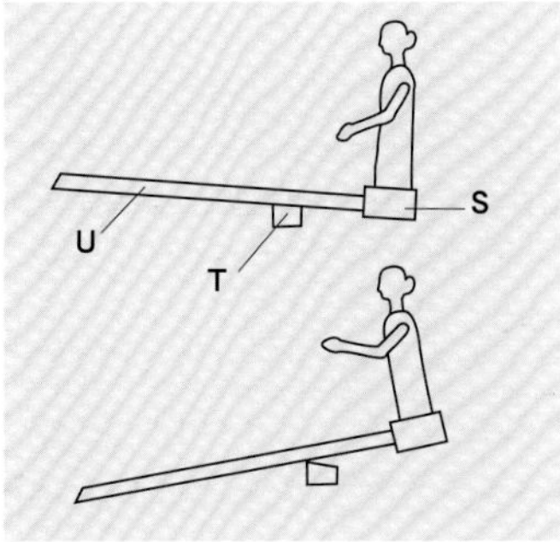

SK-11

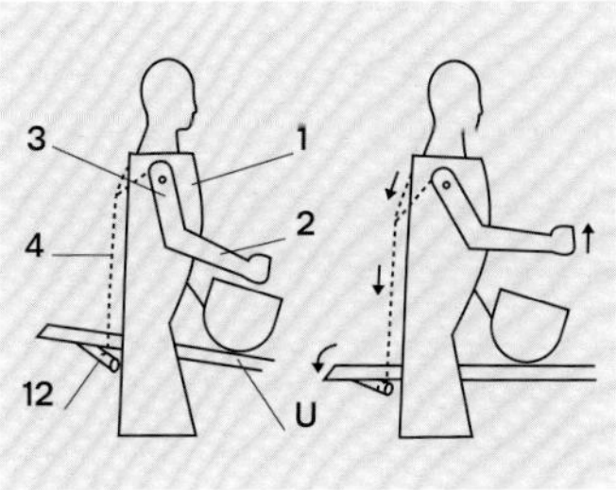

SK-12

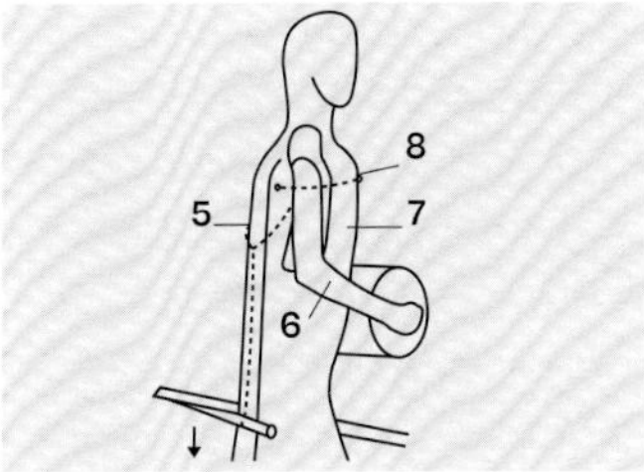

SK-13

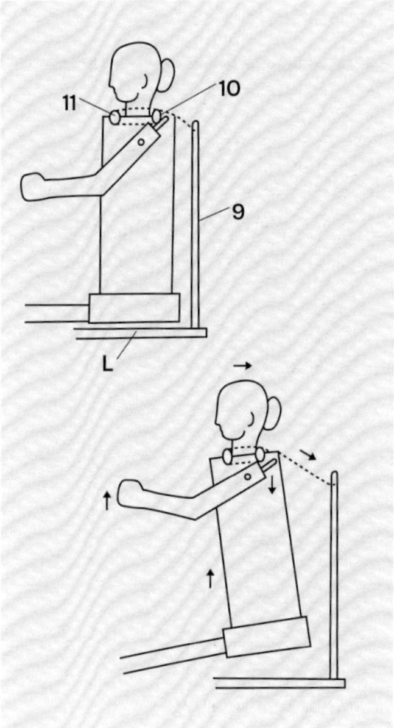

SK-14

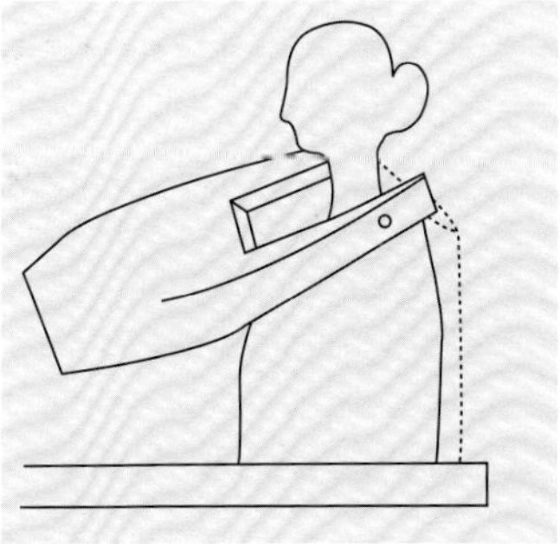
SK-15

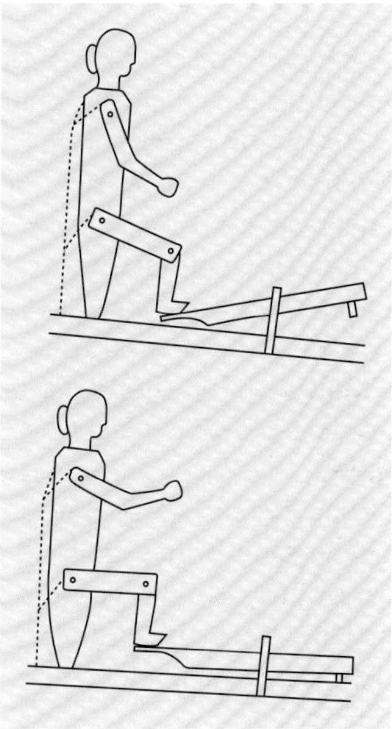
SK-16

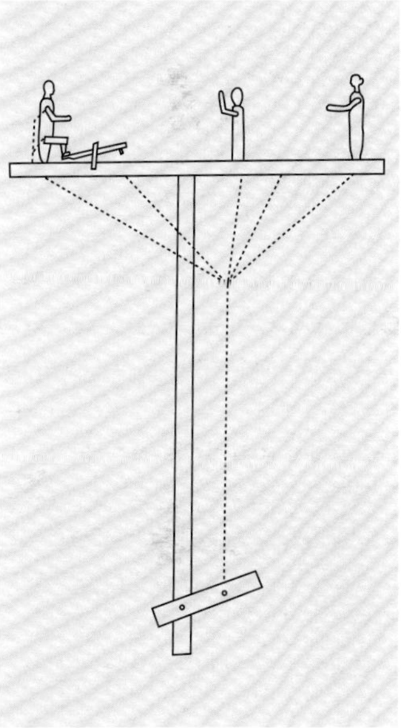
SK-17

TOOLS USED IN MAKING CHADAR BADAR

*KATARI*: Chopper for cutting wood
*LURUN*: Screw chisel for fine carving
*BHONR*: Drill bit for drilling holes
*BUTSI*: Hammer
*RUKA*: Chisel for shaping broad carving
*SANDASI*: Pliers
*TAAR*: Wire for burning holes through wood
*ALTULI*: Paintbrush
*SUI*: Needle to stitch the clothes of puppets
*KAPACHI*: Scissors

60% of the total weight of the set. Four split bamboo pieces 'H' of 4 cm length are nailed and tied to the ends of 'B' bars forming a horizontal square (SK-4). Two long flexible bamboo branches (I) (*Kanchi*) are bent and firmly tied to the diagonal corners (H), forming the vaulted frame for the coloured cloth canopy. The bamboo strips (I and K) are reinforced with long wooden erect pieces, tied at the lower part of their bases. At the corners of the frame additional bamboo branches or strips are attached (K), forming arches at each side of the frame and preventing the canopy from sagging and giving it a definite shape (SK-5).

Thin and wide wooden strips (J) are horizontally fixed with (I) and parallel to (H) at the distance of about 7.5 cm from (H). These keep the lower portion of (I) straight. The piece of cloth (*Sari* or *Chadar*) covering or hiding the mechanism extends upto lower end of (J).

THE REVOLVING STAGE (*charkha*)

The puppets are fixed on a revolving stage. In Bhulu Murmu's set the circular stage is not made of a disk or board. Instead a bamboo strip is bent and tied into a circle of 30 cm diameter (L) and is fixed around a wooden bar (M) which is fixed to two cross pieces of wood and two thick iron wires. The main wooden bar (M) takes the main load. A square wooden block (N) is inserted and firmly fixed in the centre (SK-6 and 7).

The rod (O) supporting the revolving stage is fixed with this block at its centre. This rod runs through the two round holes (bearings) (C) and (E) of the base-frame and is inserted into the pole bamboo (G). The performer is able to hold the exposed part of the rod (O) between the set of cross bars (A and B) of the base frame and make the stage revolve.

Two parallel wooden strips (P) are fixed across the bottom of the main bar (M) of the stage. Two pieces of thin rod, or thick wire (Q) run above these two strips of wood. One of their ends is inserted into one side of the circular edge (L) and the other end into the main bar (M) (SK-9). These wires therefore remain only on one side of the stage. For the convenience of our identification and description the stage is assumed to be divided into two parts by the main bar (M), mainly 'left' and 'right'. The wires (Q) run on the left side of the stage. One wooden bar (R) with grooves at its lower side (SK-8) is placed on the left side of the stage between (P) and (Q). The strips on P loosely fit into the grooves, and the wires (Q) keeps (R) in place, and allows (R) to move forward and backward along the line of (P) and (Q), i.e., towards and away from (M). The movement of (R) to the left is restricted by the circular stage frame (L) (SK-9).

Four male drummer puppets, facing right side of the stage are firmly fixed on this moving platform (R). Two on the extreme end are playing the *Nagra*, and two in the middle are playing *Madol*. Only the arms of the drummers can be moved by pulling strings. By moving (R) the drummers may be moved forward or backward. Two more male puppets — also facing right, are fixed on the central bar (M). They are the *Mataal* (drunkard) and Joker. They flap or just move their arms and heads. On the right side of the stage, is a set of eleven dancing girls that are fixed on a wooden platform (S). Two wooden pieces (U) are fixed at the left side of (S). An iron pipe (V) is fixed between two wooden pieces (U) and is parallel to (S). It is placed just over (M). A rope is inserted through the hole made at the centre of (V) for manoeuvring. This again runs through the hole in (N) (SK-10). A wooden block (T) is fixed on the stage on (P) which works as fulcrum for the bars (U). When (V) is pulled by the rope, the entire block is raised along with the dancing girls. The distance between (T) and (S) being quite small it also gives the girls a forward tilt resembling the actual dancing postures of the Santal girls.

The arms and heads of the two girls can also be moved. Now when the main rope is pulled (or released) rhythmically, the drummers beat their drums, the joker and drunkard clap and wave their arms and shake their heads, the girls tilt forward, raise their arms while their heads move back. Along with these movements, the rotation of the stage, and the forward-backward movement of the drummers create a convincing picture of a dancing scene.

MOVEMENT OF THE PUPPETS

In most cases the basic movement of the puppets is that of their hands, by pull of string the arms move upward, rising either to the front or the side. Construction of the first category is quite simple When thread (4) is pulled down the arm (2) is raised upward with the nail (or bamboo/wooden peg) working as fulcrum (SK-12). For the second category of puppets (SK-13) a long cut is made on the side of the body with a width more than that of the arm. The thread that pulls (5) the upper extreme of the arm (6) runs through the space under the arm. A tight thread (8) works as fulcrum. When the thread (5) is pulled, the arm moves up at the side of the body.

In Bhulu Murmu's set the pulling threads of all the four drummers (on a moving platform) are attached to a wooden stick hanging horizontally behind the dolls. The U-bar (SK-10) passes over a thin stick. When U is moved downwards by the manipulator who pulls the main thread attached to V, the U bars press on the stick and thus pull down the threads attached to the drummer's upper arms. So, a single pull of the main string makes the *Nagra* players (drummers) raise their hands in front of them and the *Madol* players to their side (in order to beat the drums). Other threads attached to the upper arms and/or neck of the joker and the drunkard fixed on the main platform (M of SK-10) make them clap or raise their arms and shake their heads. The set of dancing girls (*Mezhend*) are raised up with the pull of the main string; now the movement of their arms and heads is achieved by a reverse method. Short erect pieces of wood, are fixed on the outer circle of the stage. The arms of the girls are mounted on the bodies like the *Nagra* players (SK-12). The tips of their upper arms are however fixed to a single strip of wood. The heads of the girls also move in their sockets against the fulcrums. All of their necks again are attached to another strip of wood. Both horizontal strips of wood are tied to the top of the erect wood pieces (9 of SK-14) by the threads. Now when the dancers' platform is raised, the erect pieces restrict (or prohibit) the horizontal pieces from moving up, which actually means a downward pull. This action raises the hands of the dancers and moves their heads back. When the pull is released the dancers are lowered on the platform, their hands are lowered and heads are bent down.

As already explained, the actual manoeuvre is done by the pull of a thread or rope attached to a short metal piece (V) fixed between (U) bars (SK-10). The rope runs through the entire length of the supporting pole and comes out at about 10 cm above ground level. A small knob is attached to the end of the rope which is tugged by the performors toe.

## OTHER VARIATIONS

Phechu Muddy was the only puppeteer who had done daily shows on a regular basis as a solo performer. Out of necessity his set was very light and did not have the separate 'base-and stage' arrangement. The stage is made of a square frame of bamboo with one central base plank. The rest of the stage is made of thin iron rods (or thick wires) running parallel to the base plank. No arrangement for 'forward and backward movement' is made. Though his stage does not rotate, some items of rural domestic scenes are incorporated in his set.

One girl is working with the husking paddle and another is working with a winnowing fan. The dancers are, as usual, fixed on a piece of wood (semi-circular in this case), and are lifted by means of a simple lever. All of his puppets raise their hands to the front and not to the side. All manipulating strings are bunched together under the stage and tied to a single string which runs outside the bamboo stand almost to the bottom where it is tied to a paddle attached to the bamboo stand and a coloured *Sari* or *Chadar* tied around the stage covers or hides the manipulating strings and the paddle. The puppeteer holds the bamboo stand with his left hand and lowers and releases the manipulating paddle with his right toe. With his right hand he beats a simple drum, hanging waist-high from his neck, keeping beat to his songs. Phechu's set does not have a canopy. He has decorated his puppets with colourful bits of cloth (scrap he collects from tailors), giving it a gay look. Ram Hansda's set has a rotating stage, but it is lighter and less complicated than Bhulu Murmu's set. Most parts of the stage and frame are made of bamboo. The set has four legs and can stand on them. In the centre of the stage a bird is perched on a stick that raises and lowers its head and tail. It has a canopy and the usual sari covering the lower part.

Hopna Hansda's set was found in a knocked down condition. For him — an affluent peasant — the economic incentive was never a consideration. It was a matter of pleasure indulged in during the *Pujas*. He has however lost interest in his puppets since the death of his eldest son about ten years ago. Hopna — who is also an expert carpenter — made the set himself. The set had, besides the drum players and the dancers, two women engaged in husking and winnowing. Another puppet could move its jaw. Like Ram's set, it also has a bird lowering and raising its head and tail.

## CONCLUSION

The *Chadar Badar* research project was more difficult to carry out than most other craft documentation projects I have undertaken. In the first place, this form of puppetry is virtually unheard of outside its immediate area. Even the Dumka Tribal Museum and the Director of the Santal Danoo Centre in Dumka had not heard of it. I visited remote villages trying to locate puppeteers, a task made more difficult because the Santals found my interest peculiar and amusing. Initially I had only a Navasar puppeteer as my lead. When I finally tracked down more puppeteers, I was dismayed to find that I would have to wait at least six more months until September before I could hope to see them perform. When September and October arrived, however, the difficulties dissolved, and though the time was short, it was highly productive. The only goal I failed to achieve was access to historical data; I was unable to find any published or oral information on the origins and history of the form.

The photographs complete the documentation. No puppets were available for purchase, so I commissioned a complete *Chadar Badar* set for the Crafts Museum from Barkha Murmu of Danshara village, Birbhum.

1 I am most grateful to the puppeteers of Dumka, Burdwan and Birbhum districts, who offered me their hospitality and cooperation in this project. I am also indebted to Sri. Prabhas Sen for his invaluable guidance and advice, to Sri C. C. Sarkar for helping me in the actual execution of the work, to Smt. Ruby Pal Choudhuri for her keen interest in the success of the project, and to Sri Delip Chatterjee of Ahmedpur for sharing his knowledge and taking me into nearby villages. Dr. Lee Horne of the University of Pennsylvania generously agreed to edit the original report.

# FROM DUMKA TO NEW DELHI: CONVERSATIONS

Mushtak Khan
Krittika Narula
Mallika Leuzinger

Through December 2014 the Crafts Museum has been the site of several conversations. The conversations have centred on the question of how to bring the different threads of Santal culture and its particular museal forms together. In the observations offered by Ravi Kant Dwivedi as he shared his photographs and field reports, in our discussions with four Santal craftsmen, and in our telephonic exchange with two Santal women, what we have encountered is not so much a story of loss but the assimilation of new formats and materials which have become part of Santal life and which have made Santal life part of many others.

A key aspect of this documentation project was to invite Santal craftspeople and performers to be in residence at 'Shilpa Kuteer'[1] for the Crafts Demonstration Programme at the Crafts Museum. Accordingly, a field trip was organised and undertaken by Ravi Kant Dwivedi, a New Delhi-based researcher and cultural ethnographer, who has worked with the Santal community over several decades and on various occasions. He travelled to Jharkhand and West Bengal, revisiting the villages where he had conducted his earlier research.

Ravi, who trained as an artist at Kala Bhavan in Santiniketan, became interested in *Chadar Badar* puppetry[2] when he noticed an old set in a thatched hut in a village of Dumka, Jharkhand, on one of his trips to Santal Parganas in 1985. On his return to New Delhi, he started a research project for the Crafts Museum for which he conducted extensive primary research, as there was no printed material or information available on *Chadar Badar* at that time. Ever since, he has made the revival and documentation of *Chadar Badar* his main area of focus and has supported local Santal puppeteers in continuing to develop and perform their art.

Ravi's trip in 2014 was an opportunity to document contemporary Santal culture and to identify craftspeople who still practice traditional art forms. As a result of this trip, four Santal craftsmen came to New Delhi, to be in residence at the Crafts Museum. All four craftsmen are paternal cousins and belong to Navasar Village near Dumka, where their main activity is farming – growing paddy, wheat and maize. They all look forward to the weeklong celebrations in January when they perform *Chadar Badar* for the village. Each one has a specific role in the performance and specializes in playing a particular instrument while dancing to the rhythm of the movements of the puppets. Forty-seven year old Bhulu Murmu, also a puppet-maker, performs the *Madal* (hand-struck two-headed drum). Forty-year old Babudhan Murmu plays the *Tirio* (flute). Fifty-five year old Shibdhan Murmu, a grandfather of two, operates the *Chadar Badar* puppets with the tug of his foot and hands. Forty-five year old Sonadhan Murmu plays the *Nagada* or *Tamak* (single-headed kettle drum). Traditionally *Chadar Badar* performances could also include a cymbal as well as a *Banam* (one-stringed bowed lute) player.

During their stay at the Crafts Museum, Bhulu Murmu and his troupe gave several *Chadar Badar* performances in the Crafts Demonstration area. The core audience of researchers was often joined by a host of curious school children and other visitors jostling for a view. This space also became the studio in which the craftsmen set to work making puppets and various musical instruments. While the making and playing of these traditional instruments were filmed and photographed as part of the documentation initiative, the craftsmen seized the opportunity to engage with their traditions. They were able to look at the archival materials held at the Crafts Museum and even restored a *Chadar Badar* set for the Museum made by Bhulu Murmu's father, Lukhin Murmu, in 2010. The craftsmen were informed of the exhibition at the Museum Rietberg[3] and the catalogue was made available for them to see. They also attended a special screening of Deben Bhattacharya's film, *Faces of the Forest*. Inspired by these interactions, they carved a new *Banam* as well as several puppets for a making a *Chadar Badar* set at the Museum.

Given their usual work in the fields, they are rarely able to devote an entire month to carving or performing. The interactions we had, as well as the access to older artefacts and archival material stored at the Crafts Museum, encouraged them to fully immerse themselves in and reflect on their crafts.

## IN CONVERSATION

*Ravi Kant Dwivedi with Mallika Leuzinger*

Ravi spoke with familiarity and respect about everyday life documented in the photographs (p. 81, photo 1 to 8) that he brought back. Men walking to the forest to gather wood for fuel (photo 1, 2), women making brooms under the shade of a tree (photo 3, 4, 5), a boy fashioning a leaf into a musical toy for himself (photo 6, 7, 8) – all these images were for Ravi unsurprising examples of how Santals spend a lot of time outdoors and make ingenious use of locally available resources.

He also dwelt on the photographs of Santal men, and women wearing green saris and floral headdress, dancing and singing, and of villagers crowding around a *Chadar Badar* performance. These photographs attest to the continuation of the embodied and variegated

1

2

3

4

5

6

7

8

participation of Santals in communal activities, which had so impressed Ravi in 1988. He spoke at length about how Santal children learn how to play an instrument, how to dance, even how to carve wood, by observation and practice because these activities are always happening around them. Ravi, however, also confronted much that he was unfamiliar with. Ever present in his photographs from 2014 is the imbrication of plastic and other mass-produced goods in the form of jewellery, toys, brooms, and chairs. Flowers made in China took pride of place on the handlebar of a young man's bicycle. When Ravi asked this young man why he chose plastic flowers to decorate his bicycle instead of real flowers since the latter were, after all, fresh and abundant, the answer he received was that real flowers were simply not as good: they died, and would have to be replaced everyday.

Ravi faced some difficulties in his efforts to reconnect with people. Of those he hoped to meet, many had moved elsewhere, and some, like his friend the puppeteer and *Banam* maker, Barka Soren of Gargaria village, had passed away. His attempts to persuade some craftsmen to come to Delhi were fraught: several refused outright, citing other commitments such as the upcoming harvest season. Other groups, which had promised to come, cancelled at the last minute. Comparing this visit to his earlier one, Ravi felt much had changed. But he was reassured by the very warm welcome from his old friend, the *Chadar Badar* puppeteer and maker, Bhulu Murmu, in the Jharkhand village of Navasar.

Ravi had been the first researcher to document the cultural traditions in Navasar. At the time of his first trip, Bhulu Murmu was fifteen years old and had started learning *Chadar Badar* puppetry from his father. He had maintained contact with Ravi over the years. Bhulu, along with his relatives, Shibdhan Murmu, Sonadhan Murmu and Babudhan Murmu, had visited Delhi some years before, to participate in a documentation initiative of the Indira Gandhi National Centre for the Arts. They thus readily agreed to participate in the Crafts Museum's programme, and arrived in Delhi on December 1st, 2014.

IN CONVERSATION
*Bhulu Murmu and Babudhan Murmu and family with Krittika Narula*

In the course of explaining our documentation project, the craftsmen were told about the exhibition at the Museum Rietberg and shown the catalogue, which, though in German, had many photographs of individual pieces from Bengt Fosshag's *Banam* collection. Together, they examined each one and identified the *Banams* they were familiar with. That such a large collection could exist somewhere they found amazing. Babudhan Murmu said, "even though we are farmers, we would love to spend more time making these sculptures." They said they were inspired to make more *Banams* once they were back in Navasar.

On their second day, they were already carving new puppets for a *Chadar Badar* set similar to that made by Bhulu Murmu's father. In carving these new puppets, Bhulu Murmu's inspiration was the quality of carving his father had achieved in the fine puppet bust made by him in 1985, which is now in Ravi Kant Dwivedi's collection.[4] He liked the smaller scale and finer features of the old puppet (p. 84, photos 11). Unlike his father though, Bhulu leaves his puppets unpainted and relatively unadorned (p. 84, photos 12). His puppets reflect the current hairstyles sported by women when they dance: hair gathered at the back and affixed with three pins. There are little grooves on each puppet head for paper flowers (p. 85, photo 13).

They also began restoring the *Chadar Badar* set made by Bhulu's father for the Crafts Museum. They fixed the broken arms of the puppets and the joinery between them with quick, familiar movements—stringing them together with plastic fibres from the cement bags in which they carried their tools—and answered our questions without missing a beat. These older pieces acted both as inspiration as well as a link with the past. We discussed how the older *Chadar Badar* set had additional details—of paint, jewellery, and coloured paper. One puppet is an inebriated man whose head slumps wonderfully back and forth when played, a reminder that drinking is a significant part of Santal festivals. Both men and women stop work and celebrate together with dance and drink home-produced liquor.

All four felt that Bhulu Murmu's father, Lukhin Murmu, was especially skilled, explaining that it was rare and hard to chisel so finely. Bhulu Murmu insisted, however, that he could achieve the same quality if he had more time. They agreed that skill was determined by the amount of practice and the time invested in the carving. Bhulu Murmu said his father was a very dedicated and hardworking man who liked to keep himself busy. He would work for up to fifteen days to complete one *Chadar Badar* set. Wherever he went—to the fields or on a visit to someone's house—he would take along a block of wood. When he took a break or needed rest after a day's work he would start carving. Once it took him over a year to complete a *Chadar Badar* set, which is now with his family. Since there was no pressure to finish the set, he was able to achieve a very high quality. Bhulu Murmu said that now they normally take between five to eight days to make one *Chadar Badar* set. Deben Bhattacharya's film *Faces of the Forest* (1973)[5] documents Santal communities in the Purulia region in West Bengal, and the craftsmen hail from Jharkhand. Thus the screening prompted a discussion about the differences between the traditions of the two places. There are clear regional variations in dance, music and language. Jharkhandi Santals, for example, dance while holding hands in the same manner as depicted in the *Chadar Badar* sets, which is not the way it is done in Purulia. At the same time, the craftsmen pointed out that they also shared many traditions. They recognized the rice-pounding device of the Purulia Santals and identified the same beats in their music and dances.

After spending a month at the Crafts Museum, the craftsmen said they felt encouraged to communicate to their children the appreciation their craft has received beyond their own region. Though *Chadar Badar* is no longer a regular activity in the life of the community, they felt the next generation should have the choice to practice this craft just as Bhulu Murmu did.

IN CONVERSATION
*Sangita Murmu and Jashodi Murmu*
*with Krittika Narula*
Our interactions with Bhulu Murmu and Babudhan Murmu and family were extended by our conversations with the women who had stayed behind in Navasar, and in doing so, made the men's visit possible. Sangita Murmu and Jashodi Murmu could not participate in the Crafts Demonstration Programme at the Crafts Museum, as they were busy with the harvest season. A dialogue was thus initiated through a series of telephonic exchanges.

Sangita, who is Babudhan Murmu's daughter, is twenty years old and is fluent in Hindi and Santali. She stopped going to school after she completed tenth grade, and now assists her mother at home and in the fields. Her day revolves around the chores that she and her mother perform. At the time of our conversation, the task at hand was harvesting the rice.

Jashodi, Sangita's mother, is thirty-five years old. The harvest season was keeping her very busy, as she had to supervise and manage all the work with her daughter while the men of the family were away in Delhi. She talked about her daily routine which includes all the household chores — washing clothes, cooking and cleaning, as well as fetching water several times a day from a local well, which fortunately was not too far away.

For the upcoming festive season Jashodi, Sangita and other women of the household were going to make fresh mud paintings on the walls of the house (p. 83, photos 9, 10). For these paintings they collect fresh dry mud from the open fields and mix it with water. They apply this wet paste onto the walls in two stages: first, they apply a flat layer onto the wall and then, using a stick or a piece of metal, they draw out different patterns. The most popular are of flowers, fish and birds. The raised platform that is often found on the outside of a traditional Santali hut is also painted. For this, they again apply a flat layer of mud, and then draw out patterns such as lines, waves and circles,

9

10

using their fingers and strips made out of waste rubber. Such paintings are usually made during the months of November, December and January. As we spoke, the harvesting activities were drawing to a close and they were looking forward to dancing and singing at the *Sohrai* festival in the middle of January.

There was no pressure on Sangita to learn any of the Santali songs while she was growing up, but since she enjoys dancing during the *Sohrai* festival, she knows "a little bit" of Santali dance. Jashodi, on the other hand, said that she enjoyed dancing and singing the Santali songs which she had learnt while she was growing up. She sang a song that is popular at this time of the year:

*Yesterday we cleaned and bathed*
*Everyone in the village did*
*Today in our homes*
*Next to the walls within*
*We will pray*

11

12

13

14

IN CONVERSATION

*Portrait of a Puppeteer: Bhulu Murmu with Mushtak Khan*

Bhulu Murmu (photo 14, above) is a *Chadar Badar* puppeteer and puppet maker and among the last few performers of this rapidly vanishing art form. The Santals of Dumka district in Jharkhand mainly practice *Chadar Badar* puppetry. Bhulu, accompanied by the three other members of his team, participated in the Craft Demonstration Programme of the Crafts Museum, New Delhi, where I spent many hours with him.

Bhulu is around forty-seven years old. He speaks with great thought and care, never replying to questions in a hurry. He knows very little Hindi, though his fellow craftsman Babudhan Murmu speaks Hindi fluently. Bhulu lives about 25 kilometres from Dumka town in the village of Navasar, which is encircled by a small river called Noonbel. Navasar is home to a 150 families, constituting a population of nearly 1200.

The few *Jadupatua* (Patua painters) families who number in this population are an integral part of Navasar's cultural life. They are an occupational painter and storyteller community that has strong links to Santal society though they themselves are not Santal. Nitai, Ganapati and Mahapati Chitrakars are still practicing painters and provide the *Chakkhudan* ritual paintings to Santals for their funeral rites. They also make scroll paintings of Santal myths. Bhulu tells me that two other *Jadupatua*s in his village had to abandon their traditional occupation and take up other work to earn a livelihood.

Two ironsmith families are also important members of Bhulu's village. Babudhan Rana and Okil Rana are skilled ironsmiths and make fine *Kajroti* (kohl containers) and betel nutcrackers. Both these objects are essential for a Santal marriage ceremony. I asked Bhulu to tell me about Navasar's development over the years. He remembered that the first bus service from Dumka to his village was started in 1976. Now, Navasar lies on the State Highway, which goes from Dumka to Jamtada. When I asked him about other inroads India's modernity had made into village life, he informed me that the first television powered by batteries appeared in 2006, and electricity arrived in 2012. Today, six families, including a Santal household, have television sets. Most villagers are not very interested in regular TV programmes and prefer to watch feature films.

It is while on the subject of entertainment that we began to talk about *Chadar Badar.* Bhulu told me that up until around forty years ago, *Chadar Badar* puppetry was a popular form of recreation amongst the Santal community. Possessing no religious significance, nor any association with rituals or deities, it is a celebratory event. During the month of *Bhadrapada* (August-September), which follows the harvesting of maize, puppeteers visit every house in the neighbouring villages, accompanying the puppet show with singing and dancing. In return, the occupants of the houses offer grain or money. This goes on for a week, at the end of which the entire troupe enjoys a feast from their earnings, members receiving an equal share. Puppeteers also perform at a local festival called *Chhata Parab.* This takes place during the period when village fairs are organized, and provides them an opportunity to earn a little something, as well as having fun.

I asked Bhulu how he came to *Chadar Badar.* Bhulu's father, Lukhin Murmu, was a famous puppet maker and puppeteer of the region. He died about twenty-four years ago. Bhulu spoke of his father as a very good craftsman. He taught him in a way that that Bhulu described fondly as "playful", the complexity involved in making the puppets, showing him how to join them together and how to make them mobile with the help of a string. He also explained to Bhulu, who in turn explained to me, the qualities of different types of woods such as *Gamaar, Sisur, Katahal* (Jackfruit) and *Gulaij Baha* (*Champa*). Of these, the first three are good for puppet making, whereas the last one is most suitable for making a *Banam.*

Apart from Lukhin, Bhulu knows of only one other *Chadar Badar* maker who was active at the same time: Mathur Murmu, who lived in the village of Toro Pahari, some twelve kilometres from Navasar. After his death, no one has been making *Chadar Badar* in Toro Pahari, and the remaining members of his troupe now play drums during Santal weddings. Bhulu did not know whether his grandfather was also a puppet maker or not, and so the story of how his own father came to *Chadar Badar* is lost to us. Bhulu could, however, describe to me how people would commission a puppet set from his father, and also borrowed his set after the harvest season, sharing the grain they collected from the villagers as a reward for their performances with him. In 1988, Lukhin made the *Chadar Badar* set which is now in the collection of the Crafts Museum.

One of the things I gleaned from my conversations with Bhulu is that making *Chadar Badar* sets is not a traditional occupation for a family. Bhulu's father was the only son in his family and Bhulu himself had just one brother and one sister. Of the three, he was the only one interested in *Chadar Badar*, and started learning how to make it at around the age of ten. His sister never thought of doing woodwork, and indeed, no Santal woman is engaged in *Chadar Badar* making; they also do not participate in the playing of *Chadar Badar*. Bhulu's brother, meanwhile, never trained with their father to learn this work. After Lukhin Murmu's death, his puppet set became Bhulu's property.

Thereupon, Bhulu concentrated on becoming an independent *Chadar Badar* maker and player, forming his own troupe. His team members are his relatives, and accompany the show as the drummer, flute player and dancer. They proudly told me that although they sing traditional songs during the show, they have also composed their own new song. This song, which they sang for me and which I translate below, makes light of how villagers make excuses for not giving enough grain as reward to the puppeteers:

*There was much rain in the month of June–July*
*(when it was not needed),*
*No rain arrived in the month of August-September*
*(when it was much needed),*
*O Chadar Badar puppeteer!*
*What can we give you?*
*Without rain our entire paddy crop is lost.*

Bhulu is not a full-time *Chadar Badar* maker. He is a farmer, and his family is dependent on agriculture. He has only one crop of paddy, which takes six months to ripen. This means that, after harvesting, he has plenty of time for other work. He also grows maize and vegetables for his own consumption. The rest of the time he works as part time wage labour for government schemes, making roads or digging ponds. It is then that he also makes *Chadar Badar* sets. In the past few years, he has sold just three *Chadar Badar* sets. His last customer, to whom he sold a set for Rs. 3000, was from the village of Aamda Pada and not a Santal. He told me that people from other communities also participate in the *Chadar Badar* team.

When I asked Bhulu if he had seen other puppet shows, he told me that once, about twelve or fifteen years ago, he and his troupe saw a puppet show at a village fair. The show was organized in a tent and required an entry ticket. As he had witnessed the show from a distance, he could not make out what kinds of puppets were used, or how they were played. He also could not say which area of the country the puppeteers were from. But he did say that he was not impressed by the show. In his view, their own puppet show is much more enjoyable and close to the people.

It is this sense of modest pride that emerged in many of Bhulu's answers to my questions. He acknowledged that making and playing *Chadar Badar* was not enough to earn a livelihood, recounting how his friends often ask why he is "wasting time going door to door playing puppets for just a little grain or money?" or exhort him to "Do some other work that gives you more!" But, as he told me, he enjoys making and playing *Chadar Badar*, and so he can never give it up.

I would like to end on the enthusiastic comment Bhulu Murmu made. Bhulu has three sons. The youngest one goes to school, a fact, which Bhulu is very happy about. None of them, however, is learning the art of making *Chadar Badar*. Initially, Bhulu told me that perhaps he and his generation would be the last *Chadar Badar* makers. But some days later he said that coming to the Crafts Museum had been a real treat for his troupe. They had received such love and honour that he has begun to think that he should encourage his sons to learn and continue *Chadar Badar*.

1 The Crafts Museum runs a Crafts Demonstration Programme to which about 50 craftspersons are invited each month from all over the country to be in residence (at the Craftspersons' dormitory 'Shilpa Kuteer'), to demonstrate their craft and to explore new design and market opportunities. Included in this programme are performance artists, of dance, theatre, storytelling and song.

2 *Chadar Badar* is a unique type of puppetry. It is different from the string, rod, gloves and shadow puppetry that are popular in India. The *Chadar Badar* set, which is made of wood, bamboo and fabric and operated by a simple mechanical principle, consists of wooden puppets that, when played, mimic Santal dance and musical performance.

3 In November 2013, the Museum Rietberg acquired a large number of Indian stringed instruments from the illustrator and graphic designer Bengt Fosshag, a private collector in Rüsselsheim, Germany. The Museum organized 'Sculpted Sound: Stringed Instruments from India' (4 September 2014–19 April 2015) with 92 pieces from the collection.

4 This puppet was documented and photographed along with other archival material at the Crafts Museum in December 2014.

5 Researcher, anthropologist, and documentary filmmaker Deben Bhattacharya in *Faces of the forest: Santals of Bengal* (produced by Seabourne Enterprises Film Production, 1973) explores the social habits, religious ceremonies, and the daily life of the Santal community in Belpahari Village, West Midnapore, West Bengal.

# PHOTOGRAPHS FROM 2014
Ravi Kant Dwivedi
Sudhanshu Shandilya

Ravi Kant Dwivedi (b. 1954) undertook in 2014 a field trip to Jharkhand and West Bengal to document Santal traditions. In Jharkhand he visited Modidih, Labandia and Panduba (District Godda) and Navasar, Kukurtupa and Hatiapathar (District Dumka), and in West Bengal, he visited the villages of Bannab Gram, Uttar Shiala, Bonerpukur Danga, Gargaria, Surull and Patharghata (District Birbhum). His earlier field trip in 1988 covered many of these villages in the two states.

Sudhanshu Shandilya (b. 1984) is a young photographer based in New Delhi. He documented the *Chadar Badar* puppetry troupe in residence at the Crafts Museum in December 2014. The photographs show Bhulu Murmu (*Chadar Badar* maker), Shibdhan Murmu (*Chadar Badar* performer), Sonadhan Murmu (accompanist musician) and Babudhan Murmu (accompanist musician).

Myth of the Origin of the Santals
(*Santal Janam Katha*),
by Harish Chandra Chitrakar
pigment on paper, 536 × 35 cm
Crafts Museum, New Delhi, 2014

The *Jadupatuas* are traditional painters who depict the Santal tribal myth, *Santal Janam Katha* or 'Origin of the Universe'. The following is a version of this myth in a painting by Harish Chandra Chitrakar, based on the narration of Baul Chitrakar at the Crafts Museum, in December 2014. Translation by Ravi Kant Dwivedi.

Many million years ago there was water everywhere and everything was submerged underneath. The Supreme gods *Marang Buru*, *Jaher Era* and *Sing Bonga* decided to rescue life. *Marang Buru* brought two cows from heaven. From their saliva two moths were born. When the moths grew, they turned into birds. The birds kept on flying because there was water everywhere and no place to sit and rest. *Marang Buru* created a fish, a crab and a prawn and asked them to bring mud from *Pataal* (the third and lowest level of the universe) and settle it on the water. But they failed. Then he created the earthworm. The earthworm managed to settle a small quantity of mud on the water. *Marang Buru* then created a tortoise so it could float on the water, and the earthworm could put the mud on its back. But it was difficult for the tortoise to keep floating endlessly. So *Marang Buru* asked *Shesh Naag* (the Ultimate Snake) to spread its hood, so the tortoise could rest on it. This is how the Earth was created. The birds laid two eggs. From these, two humans – a male and a female – *Pilchu Haram* and *Pilchu Budhi*, were born. They were the first Santals.

*Pilchu Haram* and *Pilchu Budhi* had seven sons and eight daughters. Finding it difficult to manage so many children, they approached *Marang Buru* for advice. *Marang Buru* told *Pilchu Haram* and *Pilchu Budhi* to go to Khararai forest and collect some *Bakar* (a fermenting agent) to prepare *Hanrhiya* (rice beer) and call him when the beer was ready. They followed instructions, but then forgot to call *Marang Buru*. Instead, they consumed large quantities of beer themselves, got drunk and started beating each other. *Marang Buru* rushed in to settle the matter. *Pilchu Budhi* was reluctant to stay with her husband. *Marang Buru* asked the couple to separate. He told *Pilchu Haram* to take the seven sons, and *Pilchu Budhi* to take the eight daughters. *Pilchu Budhi* and the girls went to Surhur forest while *Pilchu Haram* settled with the boys at Khararai forest.

Years passed. The children grew up separately and reached adulthood. One day the boys went to hunt in a forest, and the girls arrived at the same forest to gather fruits and vegetables. The boys saw the girls singing and swinging under a Banyan tree. The boys and girls met and became friends. They started meeting every day and fell in love.

One day the seven boys married seven of the girls by smearing dust into the parting of their hair. The eldest girl, *Kanta Budhi*, did not marry. They indulged in dancing and singing. After some time had passed and the boys and girls did not return home, *Pilchu Haram* went out to look for the boys. He reached the forest the same time as *Pilchu Budhi*, who had come to look for the girls. The two met after 12 years and recognized each other. They were surprised to know that their own children, who were brothers and sisters, had married each other. *Marang Buru* appeared, approved their marriage and blessed the couples. He divided the seven couples into seven sects and clans and asked the eldest unmarried sister to look after the pregnant mothers and the newborn babies. He renamed her *Marang Dei* and asked everybody to worship her during the Bandhana festival. The men went to the forest to hunt. The elders gathered to make a code of conduct for the community. They sat on lotus leaves and dictated that there will be no marriages between brothers and sisters or within the same clan.

Time passed and the population increased. There was a man named *Gadai Marandi* who was very handsome and with long hair. He also had the disease elephantitis, where the limbs swell. A girl from the *Kishku* clan fell in love with him because of his handsome head of hair and wanted to marry him. But when she saw his swollen legs she refused him. This enraged *Gadai Marandi* so much that he cut off her head. After this, marriages between *Kishkus* and *Marandis* became taboo and the two clans became arch rivals.

The myth generally ends with the ritual of *Chakkhudan*, performed by the *Chitrakar, Jadau Guru*. When *Pilchu Haram* and *Pilchu Budhi* died, they were cremated so their souls could rest in peace. Their siblings went to *Marang Buru*, who was taking a bath. They asked him how the dead might achieve salvation of the soul. *Marang Buru* then created the *Chitrakar, Jadau Guru* (*Jadupatua*), from the rubbings of his body and bestowed upon him the task of guiding the departed souls to Heaven through the ritual of *Chakkhudan*. The journey of the soul is made smooth if the family of the deceased donates to *Jadau Guru*, any used objects of the deceased – like cloth, utensils, umbrella, or a hen or goat, and some money.

On *Sohrai* festival, the Santals worship cows and bulls as gratitude for their contribution to the work on the land. The Santals used to wear the sacred thread. One day, the seven sons of *Pilchu Haram* left their sacred threads on the grass when they went to the pond to bathe. *Dhaimana*, the snake, took away all the seven threads. After this incident, Santals stopped wearing the sacred thread and kill the *Dhaimana* snake whenever they see it.

Once upon a time there were seven brothers who lived with their sister. One day the sister cut her finger, and the blood ran down onto the vegetables she was preparing. The brothers found the meal very tasty and thought that if her blood alone was so delicious, her flesh would be even more so. So they decided to kill their sister and eat her.

The youngest brother, dearly fond of his sister, found it impossible to eat of her flesh and hid his portion in a termite hill. Time passed and a tree grew on this spot with beautiful white scented blossom. The tree made a wondrous sound.

One day, a wandering *yogi* (ascetic) heard the sound and marvelled at it. He decided to cut a branch from the tree to carve a musical instrument. This instrument, made from the wood of the *Champa* tree, is the *Dhodro Banam*.

1

2

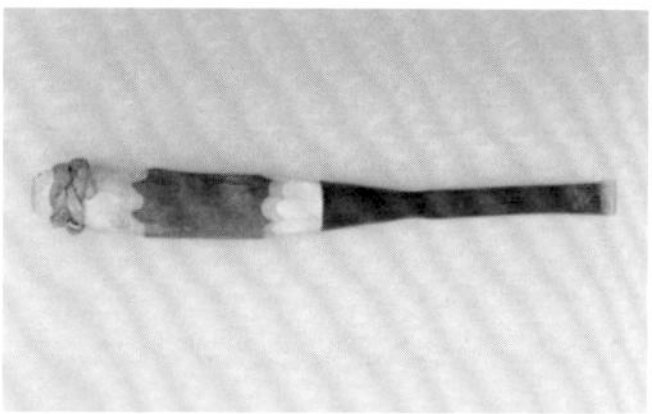

3

4

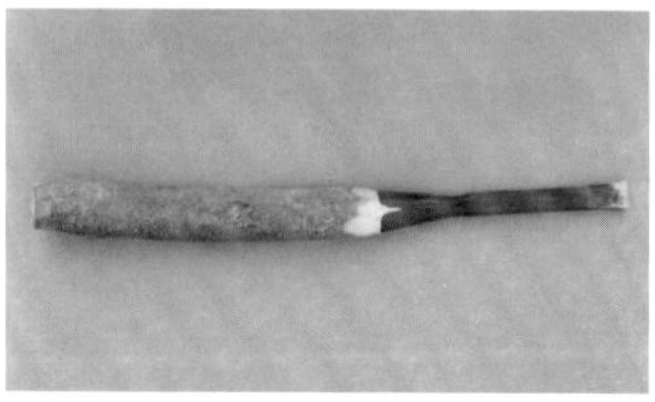

5

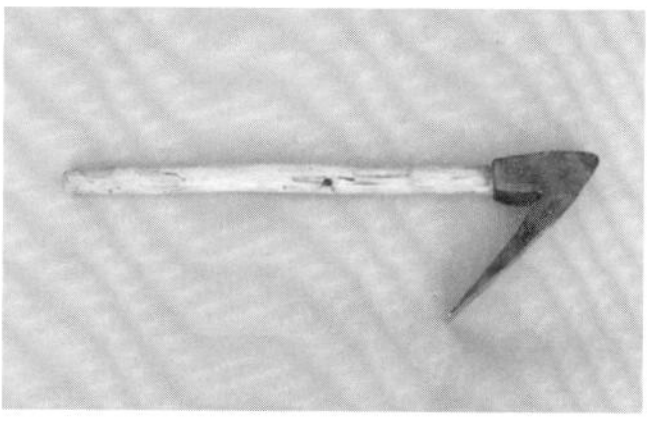

6

7

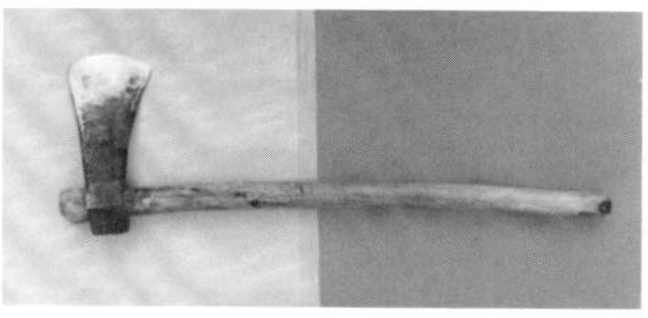

8

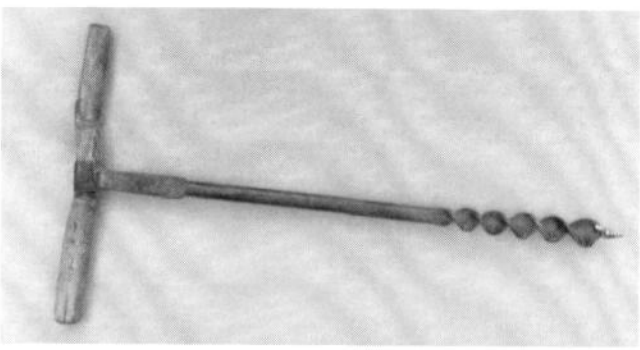

9

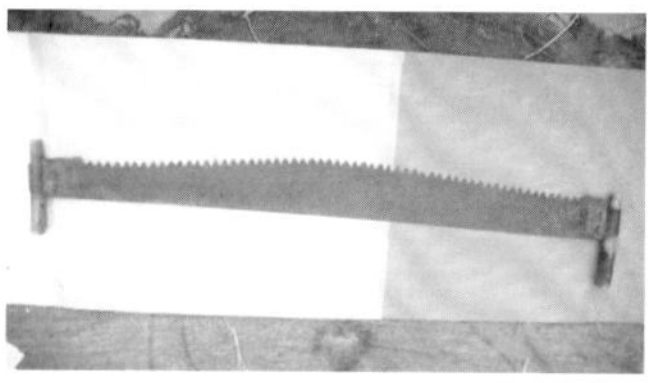

10

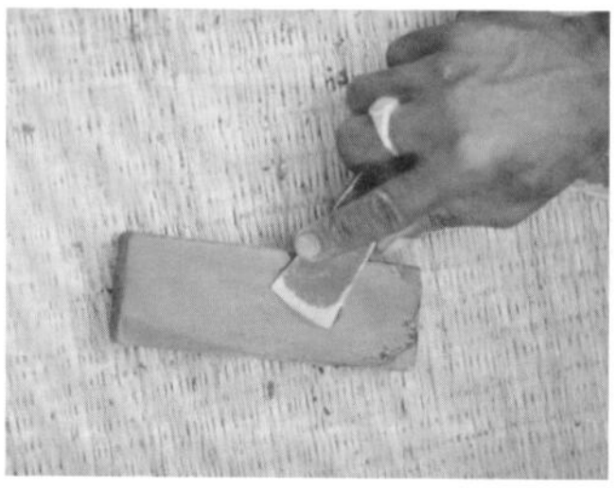

11

12

13

14

15

16

17

18

19

20

PHOTO DOCUMENTATION OF *BANAM* MAKING
JAYASRI BANERJEE

TOOLS REQUIRED FOR MAKING A *BANAM*

1. *Banki*: for cleaning animal skin. Iron with wood handles.

2. *Badari*: for cutting animal skin. Iron with wood handles.

3–4. *Chong Batali*, also called *Kund Batali*: for scraping the inside of a log. Resembles a long spoon. Iron with wood handle.

5. *Batali*: for cutting the inside of a log at the initial stage of making a *Banam*. Iron with wood handle.

6. *Baslo*: for scraping and smoothening the outer surface of a log.

7. *Haturhi* (Bengali): Hammer for hitting the *Batali* or *Chong Batali* when scraping the inside of a log.

8. *Kurhul* (Bengali): Axe. Iron with wood handle.

9. *Agar*: for making holes to fix pegs.

10. *Karat* (Bengali): Saw.

11. *Shan Pathar*: type of stone used to sharpen tools.

12. *Pata*: small platform made from a rare wood, *Banali*. Animal skin is placed on this for scraping and cleaning.

MATERIALS REQUIRED FOR MAKING *BANAM*

13. *Khol*: the wooden shell of the *Banam* is made from a thick branch of any soft wood tree, like *Chhatim*.

Goatskin: unprocessed goatskin is used for making the *Chhauni* on the *Banam*.

Resin: this is applied on the thread fixed on the *Banam*.

*Sadom*: a kind of silk thread used for fixing in the *Banam*.

MAKING VARIOUS PARTS OF *BANAM*

14. Making the *Khol* of the *Banam*.

A branch of approximate length 80 cm is cut with a *Kurhul* and cleaned.

15. Before this piece of wood is scraped to make the *Banam* shell, a *Badari* is used to mark the wood to determine the various sections which are not equal in size.

16–24. With the *Chong Batali* and *Baslo*, four sections are cut in the *Banam* shell based on the following measurements:

Section 1
16 cm (length) × 10 cm (width)

Section 2
20 cm (length) × 12.5 cm (width)

Section 3
19 cm (length) × 9 cm (width)

Section 4
19 cm (length) × 11 cm (width)

25–26. With *Batali* and *Chong Batali* these four sections are scraped.

27–28. The final look.

29. The edge of section 1 of the shell of the *Banam* is smoothened by the large *Badari* to fix the *Chhauni* on it. A hole is made in the middle of the wooden partition between Sections 1 and 2. The second section of the shell is hollowed to enhance the resonance of the

21

22

23

24

25

26

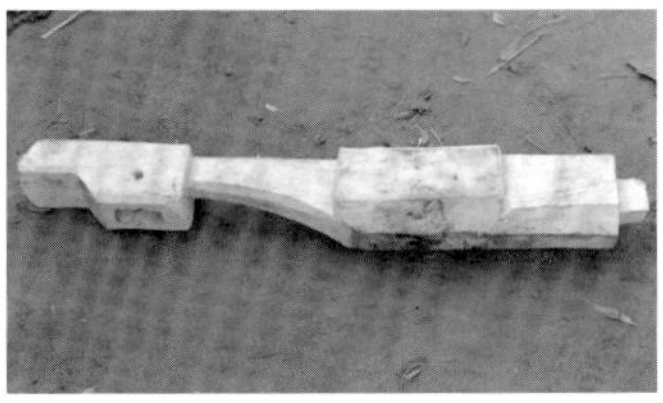
27

28

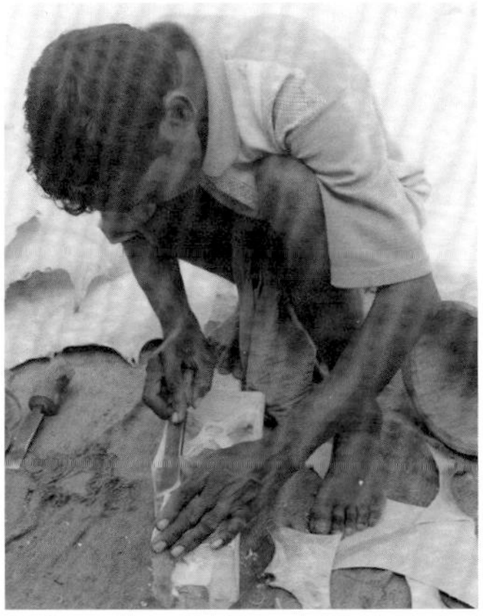
29

30

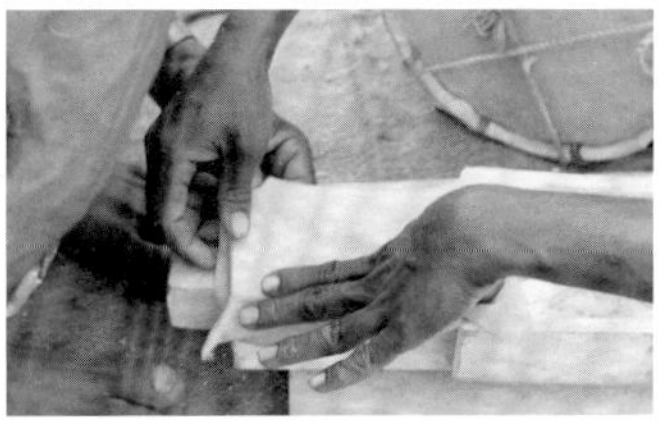
31

32

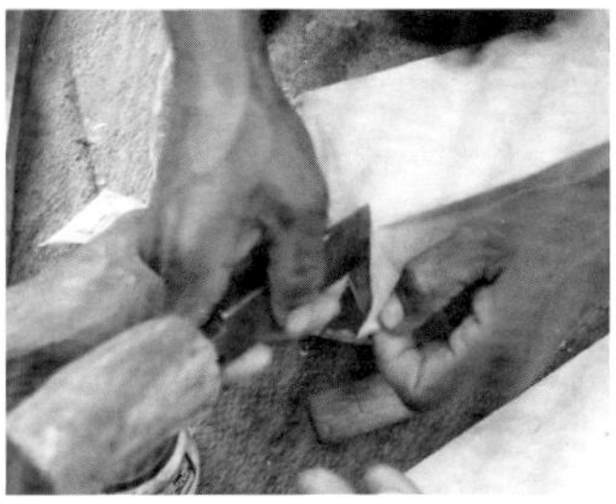
33

34

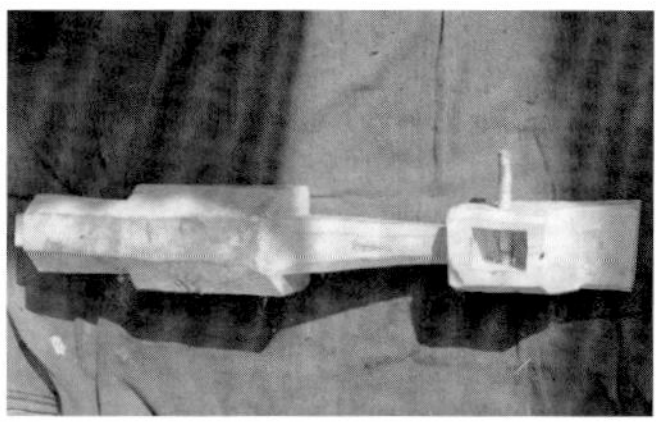
35

36

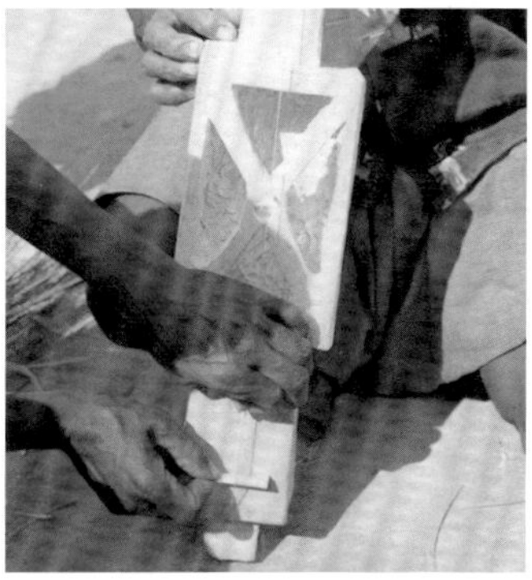
37

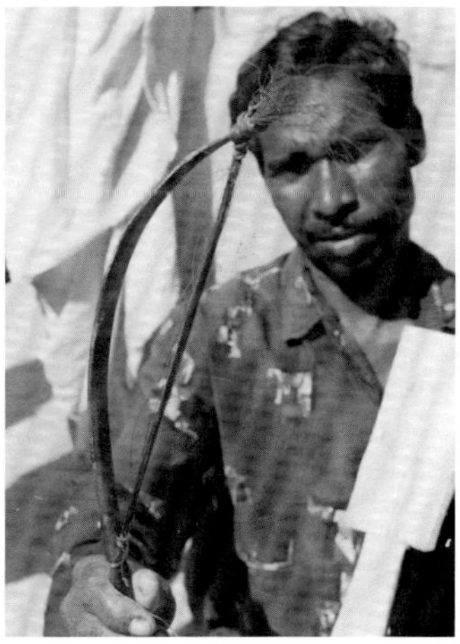
38

instrument. Another hole is made by an *Agar* on the top of Section 4 to take the playing thread inside to tie it to the peg. The inside of all four sections have wooden partitions.

FIXING *CHHAUNI*

30. The area on which the *Chhauni* is to be fixed is examined a final time with the fingers to ensure there is no roughness. The goat skin of the *Chhauni* is then scraped to remove any hair or remains of flesh. It is soaked in water for about an hour. After all water has dripped off the skin, it is placed on the mouth of Section 1 of the shell to check if the size is as per required measurement.

32. The skin of the *Chhauni* is then fixed tightly with adhesive. In the past, small wooden nails were used.

33. The extra portion of the skin is trimmed with a *Badari* and three holes are made in the lower portion of the *Chhauni* for better resonance.

34–35. Fixing the Peg. By the side of Part 4 a hole is made to fix the peg. With this peg a particular kind of thread is tied for playing the instrument.

36. Fixing the Thread. First, a long piece of *Sadam* (a kind of silken thread) is twisted firmly. It is then rubbed with resin, tied and then taken over the wooden shell of the *Banam*. This is finally taken through the small hole on the top of Section 4 and tied with the peg.

37. Fixing the Bridge. A small piece of wood is cut and loosely kept on the *Chhauni* under the thread.

38. Stage 6 – Making the *Banam Aah* (Bow). A piece of bamboo is cleaned and curved to make the *Banam Aah* and a few strands of thread are firmly tied with it. The process of making the *Banam* ends with the completion of this stage.

Photo documentation and explicatory notes on The System of Making *Banam* of the Santals is part of a Project on 'Musical Instruments of Adivasis of Jungle Mahal – Study of a Tradition in Transition' (1998–2000) by Jayasri Banerjee, supported by The India Foundation for the Arts, Bangalore, and Sangeet Natak Akademi, New Delhi.

Carriage and Figures
81 × 3 × 13 cm
Verrier Elwin Collection
National Museum, New Delhi
Inv. No. 65.51

Horses and Figures
83 × 14 × 11 cm
Verrier Elwin Collection
National Museum, New Delhi
Inv. No. 64.1296

Couple with a Child
80 × 16 × 7.5 cm
Verrier Elwin Collection
National Museum, New Delhi
Inv. No. 64.1291

Figure
61.5 × 13 × 9.5 cm
Rietberg-Kreis Acquisition
Museum Rietberg, Zurich
Inv. No. 2014.20

Masked Man
53 × 15 × 7 cm
Rietberg-Kreis Acquisition
Museum Rietberg, Zurich
Inv. No. 2014.21

Tall Man
71.5 × 12 × 10.5 cm
Rietberg-Kreis Acquisition
Museum Rietberg, Zurich
Inv. No. 2014.22

Man
51.5 × 18.5 × 5 cm
Rietberg-Kreis Acquisition
Museum Rietberg, Zurich
Inv. No. 2014.10

Pegbox with two Ears
70 × 13 × 13 cm
Bengt Fosshag Donation
Museum Rietberg, Zurich
Inv. No. 2014.19

Head with striking Face
82 × 17 × 12 cm
Rietberg-Kreis Acquisition
Museum Rietberg, Zurich
Inv. No. 2014.25

Female Body
61 × 18 × 11 cm
Rietberg-Kreis Acquisition
Museum Rietberg, Zurich
Inv. No. 2014.23

Young Woman
61.5 × 18.5 × 11 cm
Rietberg-Kreis Acquisition
Museum Rietberg, Zurich
Inv. No. 2014.9

Beautiful Head of a Woman
76 × 10.5 × 12 cm
Rietberg-Kreis Acquisition
Museum Rietberg, Zurich
Inv. No. 2014.24

Woman
88 × 16 × 13 cm
Bengt Fosshag Donation
Museum Rietberg, Zurich
Inv. No. 2014.26

Woman with Figure
on her Head
97 × 14 × 12 cm
Rietberg-Kreis Acquisition
Museum Rietberg, Zurich
Inv. No. 2014.27

Head with a Monkey
68 × 12.5 × 10.5 cm
Rietberg-Kreis Acquisition
Museum Rietberg, Zurich
Inv. No. 2014.28

Figure with open Legs
77 × 14 × 11 cm
Rietberg-Kreis Acquisition
Museum Rietberg, Zurich
Inv. No. 2014.35

Small Head of a Woman
68 × 18 × 12 cm
Bengt Fosshag Donation
Museum Rietberg, Zurich
Inv. No. 2014.36

Green Man
89 × 14.5 × 18 cm
Bengt Fosshag Donation
Museum Rietberg, Zurich
Inv. No. 2014.42

Woman with metallic Eyes
77 × 32 × 18 cm
Rietberg-Kreis Acquisition
Museum Rietberg, Zurich
Inv. No. 2014.5

Two Heads of Women
72 × 16.5 × 18.5 cm
Bengt Fosshag Donation
Museum Rietberg, Zurich
Inv. No. 2014.44

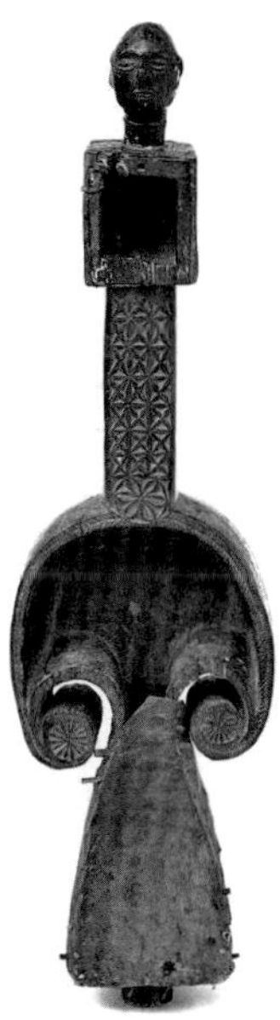

Two Riders
58 × 8 × 9 cm
Bengt Fosshag Donation
Museum Rietberg, Zurich
Inv. No. 2014.62

Two Dancers
80 × 14 × 16.5 cm
Rietberg-Kreis Acquisition
Museum Rietberg, Zurich
Inv. No. 2014.45

Two Figures
67.5 × 20 × 15.5 cm
Bengt Fosshag Donation
Museum Rietberg, Zurich
Inv. No. 2014.48

Adam and Eva
68.5 × 13.5 × 8.5 cm
Bengt Fosshag Donation
Museum Rietberg, Zurich
Inv. No. 2014.43

Two sitting Women
73 × 15.5 × 9.5 cm
Rietberg-Kreis Acquisition
Museum Rietberg, Zurich
Inv. No. 2014.47

Two Men and one Face
80 × 14 × 16 cm
Rietberg-Kreis Acquisition
Museum Rietberg, Zurich
Inv. No. 2014.46

Three Women
82.5 × 13 × 16.5 cm
Bengt Fosshag Donation
Museum Rietberg, Zurich
Inv. No. 2014.51

Three Women on four Pillars
90.5 × 14 × 15 cm
Bengt Fosshag Donation
Museum Rietberg, Zurich
Inv. No. 2014.65

Three Men
82 × 16 × 16 cm
Bengt Fosshag Donation
Museum Rietberg, Zurich
Inv. No. 2014.49

Dancing Warriors
84.5 × 13 × 13 cm
Rietberg-Kreis Acquisition
Museum Rietberg, Zurich
Inv. No. 2014.56

Three Figures and
three Horses
84 × 14.5 × 12.5 cm
Rietberg-Kreis Acquisition
Museum Rietberg, Zurich
Inv. No. 2014.61

Three Dancers with a Snake
95.5 × 17.5 × 16 cm
Bengt Fosshag Donation
Museum Rietberg, Zurich
Inv. No. 2014.63

Two Riders and two Figures
73 × 15 × 14.5 cm
Rietberg-Kreis Acquisition
Museum Rietberg, Zurich
Inv. No. 2014.60

Dancers with Skulls
83 × 12.5 × 12.5 cm
Rietberg-Kreis Acquisition
Museum Rietberg, Zurich
Inv. No. 2014.55

Four Figures
78 × 22 × 15 cm
Bengt Fosshag Donation
Museum Rietberg, Zurich
Inv. No. 2014.50

Four Women
76 × 15 × 15 cm
Bengt Fosshag Donation
Museum Rietberg, Zurich
Inv. No. 2014.54

Four Elephant Riders
82.5 × 17.5 × 10.5 cm
Rietberg-Kreis Acquisition
Museum Rietberg, Zurich
Inv. No. 2014.64

Two Riders and two Figures
73 × 30 × 12 cm
Rietberg-Kreis Acquisition
Museum Rietberg, Zurich
Inv. No. 2014.7

Four Men
73 × 17.5 × 14 cm
Rietberg-Kreis Acquisition
Museum Rietberg, Zurich
Inv. No. 2014.59

Four dancing Women
and three Drummers
79.8 × 22.5 × 8 cm
Rietberg-Kreis Acquisition
Museum Rietberg, Zurich
Inv. No. 2014.6

Dancers with an Elephant
93.5 × 18 × 12.5 cm
Rietberg-Kreis Acquisition
Museum Rietberg, Zurich
Inv. No. 2014.8

Five Women
78.5 × 16 × 13.5 cm
Bengt Fosshag Donation
Museum Rietberg, Zurich
Inv. No. 2014.53

Four dancing Women
and three Drummers
85 × 22 × 12.5 cm
Rietberg-Kreis Acquisition
Museum Rietberg, Zurich
Inv. No. 2014.52

Women with a Man
91 × 17 × 13 cm
Rietberg-Kreis Acquisition
Museum Rietberg, Zurich
Inv. No. 2014.57

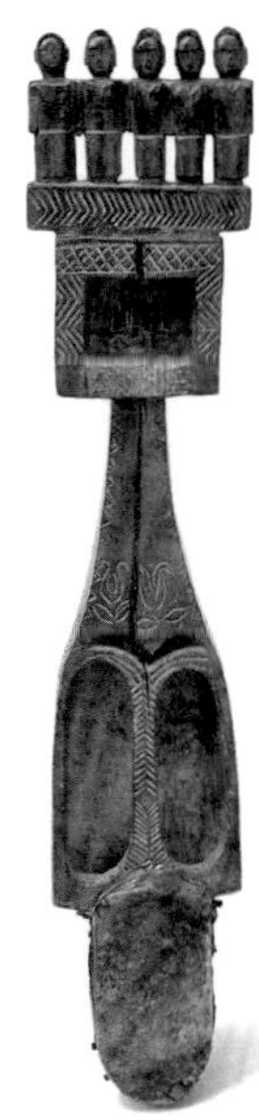

Dancers with a Musician
86 × 19 × 16 cm
Bengt Fosshag Donation
Museum Rietberg, Zurich
Inv. No. 2014.58

BIBLIOGRAPHY


Andersen, Peter B.; Carrin, Marine; Soren, Santosh K., *From Fire Rain to Rebellion: Reasserting Ethnic Identity through Narrative*, New Delhi, Manohar, 2011.

Archer, William George, *The hill of flutes: life, love, and poetry in tribal India. A Portrait of the Santals*, Pittsburgh, University of Pittsburgh Press, 1974.

Aubert, Laurent, 'La vièle-cheval et le luth-singe', *Bulletin annuel du Musée d'ethnographie de la ville de Genève*, 1986, p. 27–51.

Aubert, Laurent, 'Comment exposer la musique et que lui faire dire?', Desroches, Monique (ed.), *Mise en scène des territoires musicaux: tourisme, patrimoine et performance*, Montréal, 2011, p. 13–40.

Aubert, Laurent, 'Nouveaux objets, nouveaux enjeux: repenser l'ethnomusicologie', Bouët, Jacques; Solomos, Makis (eds.), *Musique et globalisation: musicologie – ethnomusicology*, Actes du colloque Musique et globalisation, Paris, 2011, p. 87–106.

Aubert, Laurent, 'La saveur des émotions dans l'esthétique indienne', *La saveur des arts. De l'Inde moghole à Bollywood*, Genève, MEG, Gollion, Infolio, 2011, p. 32–45.

Banerjee, Jayasri, 'Adivasi music and the public stage', *Indian Folklife*, January 2002, V. 1, 3, p. 16–17. http://www.indianfolklore.org/journals/index.php/IFL/article/view/646/792

Beltz, Johannes, 'Schöne Laute – Klingende Skulpturen: Eine Ausstellungsankündigung aus dem Museum Rietberg, Zürich', *Masala*, Newsletter Virtuelle Fachbibliothek Südasien, 2014, V. 9, No. 1, p. 25–31.

Beltz, Johannes; Mallebrein, Cornelia, *Elefanten, schaukelnde Götter und Tänzer in Trance, Bronzekunst aus dem heutigen Indien*, Zurich, 2012.

Beltz, Johannes; Celio-Scheurer, Marie-Eve (eds.), *Klang Körper. Saiteninstrumente aus Indien*, Zurich, Museum Rietberg, 2014.

Bhattacharya, Dilip, *Musical instruments of tribal India*, New Delhi, Manas Publications, 1999.

Bodding, Paul Olaf, *Materials for a Santali Grammar I*, Dumka, 1922.

Bodding, Paul Olaf, *A chapter of Santal Folklore*, Oslo, 1924.

Bodding, Paul Olaf, *Santal Folk Tales*, Oslo, Cambridge, Mass., H. Ashehoug & Co., Harvard University Press, 1925-1929, 3 V.

Bodding, Paul Olaf, *Santal Medicine and connected Folklore*, 1925–40, 3 V.

Bodding, Paul Olaf, *A Santal Dictionary*, Oslo, Det Norske Videnskaps Akademi, 1932–1936, 5 V.

Bodding, Paul Olaf, *Santal Riddles and Witchcraft among the Santals*, Oslo, A. W. Broggers, 1940.

Bodding, Paul Olaf; Bompas, Cecil Henry, *Folklore of the Santal* Parganas, London, D. Nutt, 1909. http://www.gutenberg.org/etext/11938

Bohlman, Philip Vilas, *World Music: A Very Short Introduction*, New York, Oxford University Press, 2002.

Bor, Joep, *The Voice of the Sarangi: An illustrated history of bowing in India*, New Delhi, 1987.

Borer, Philippe, 'Le corde di Paganini', *Atti del Convegno Internazionale di Liuteria* – Recupero e conservation del violino 'Guarneri del Gesù' (1743) detto 'Cannone', Genoa, 2004, p. 85–98.

Bouez, Serge; Carrin-Bouez, Marine, 'Le Mythe de Création Santal', *Asie du Sud-Est et Monde Insulindien*, 1975, 5, p. 124–152.

Carrin, Marine, 'The Hinduization of the tribal indigenous groups in India', Jacobsen, K.; Basu, H. (eds.), *Brill's Encyclopaedia of Hinduism*, Leiden, Brill, 2012, V. 3, p. 588–604.

Carrin, Marine, 'Performing Indigeneity on a Sacred Hill: Logo Buru', Ciocca, R.; Das Gupta, S. (eds.), *Out of Hidden India: Adivasi histories, stories, visualities and performances*, Anglistica, Universita degli Studi di Napoli l'Orientale, in press.

Carrin, Marine, *Le Parler des Dieux: le Discours Rituel Santal entre l'Oral et l'Ecrit (Inde)*, Nanterre, Société d'Ethnologie, in press.

Carrin-Bouez, Marine, 'L'ascension des filandres. Chants des initiés Santal', *Cahiers de littérature orale*, 1978, 3, p. 89–138.

Carrin-Bouez, Marine, 'Le retour de l'origine: mythe, chant et rite dans une fête santal', *ASEMI*, 1979, 20 (2, 3, 4), p. 87–117.

Carrin-Bouez, Marine, 'La Fleur et l'os: Symbolisme et rituel chez les Santal', *Cahier de l'Homme*, Paris, EHESS, 1986.

Carrin-Bouez, Marine, 'La bière de riz santal: ferment et monnaie du rite', *Informations sur les sciences sociales*, 1987, 26 (3), p. 611–632.

Chakrabarti, Byomkes, *A Comparative Study of Santali and Bengali*, Kolkata, KP Bagchi, 1994.

Charkraborty, Uptal; Faivre, Jean-Baptiste, 'Rouleaux peints des chitrakars ou jadupatuas des Santal Parganas-Etat du Bihar (Inde)', *Objets et Mondes*, 1980, V. 20, 3.

Chattopadhyaya, Kamaladevi, *Tribalism in India*, New Delhi, 1978.

Chaudhury, A. B., *State Formation among Tribals. A Quest for Santal Identity*, New Delhi, Gyan Pub. House, 1993.

Choksi, Nishaant, *Scripting Autonomy: Script, code and performance among Santali speakers in Eastern India*, unpublished thesis, University of Michigan, 2014.

Culshaw, W. J., *Tribal Heritage. A Study of the Santals*, London, Lutterworth Press, 1949.

Daniélou, Alain, *Inde du Nord. Les traditions musicales*, Paris, Buchet-Chastel, 1966.

Daniélou, Alain, 'Religious Music in the Twentieth Century', *Music in a changing World*, Paris, Neuchâtel, 1974, p. 227–237.

Daniélou, Alain, 'Südasien', *Musikgeschichte in Bildern*, Leipzig, Deutscher Verlag für Musik, 1978.

Das, N. K.; Misra, Kamal K. (eds.), *Dissent, Discrimination and Dispossession. Tribal Movements in Contemporary India*, Bhopal, IGRMS, Manohar, 2014.

Deva, Bigamudre Chaitanya, *Musical instruments*, New Delhi, National Book Trust, 1977.

Deva, Bigamudre Chaitanya, *Musical Instruments of India. Their History and Development*, Kolkata, Firma KLM, 1978.

Devy, G.N. (ed.), *Tribal Arts in India. The National Inventory of Tribal Museums*, Vadodara, Purva Prakash Publications, 2012.

Dietrich, Wolf; Fosshag, Bengt, *Aussereuropäische Lauten. Werkzeug und Kunstwerk*, Frankfurt/M., Verlag Brigitte Fosshag, 1992.

Doshi, Saryu, *Tribal India: Ancestors, Gods and Spirits*, Mumbai, Marg Publications, 1992.

Duyker, Edward, *Tribal Guerillas: the Santals of West Bengal and the Naxalite Movement*, New Delhi, Oxford University Press, 1987.

Elwin, Verrier, *Myths of Middle India*, Oxford, Oxford University Press, 1949.

Elwin, Verrier, *The Tribal Art of Middle India. A Personal Record*, London, Oxford University Press, 1951.

Fosshag, Bengt, 'Die Sarinda und ihre Verwandten', *Zeitschrift für Geschichte der arabisch-islamischen Wissenschaften*, 1997, 11, p. 291–306.

Fosshag, Bengt, 'The Lutes of the Santal', *Tribal Arts*, 1996, Autumn, p. 62–72.

Fosshag, Bengt, 'Anthropomorphe Darstellungen an Lauteninstrumenten', Koch, Lars-Christian; Vogels, Raimund (eds.), *Mit Haut und Haar. Die Welt der Lauteninstrumente*, Stuttgart, Linden-Museum, Staatliches Museum für Völkerkunde, 1996, p. 91–96.

von Fürer-Haimendorf, Christoph, *Tribes of India: The Struggle for Survival*, Berkeley, University of California Press, 1982. von Führer-Haimendorf, Christoph, *Die nackten Nagas. Dreizehn Monate unter Kopfjägern Indiens*, Leipzig, F. A. Brockhaus Verlag, 1939.

Ghosh, Parul; Vanshi-Parampara ke Samvahak, 'Pandit Pannalal Ghosh', Chayanat 89, 2000, p. 5–23. Translated from Bengali to Hindi by Madanlal Vyas, *Clements, Carl J., Pannalal Ghosh and the Bansuri in the Twentieth Century*, unpublished thesis, New York, The City University of New York, 2010.

Gupta, Sankar Sen, *The Patas and the Patuas of Bengal*, Kolkata, Indian Publications, 1973.

Hansda, Gokul; Kämpchen, Martin (eds.), *Mein Liebling spielt die Flöte. Lieder des indischen Santal-Stammes*, Boppard am Rhein, Fidula Verlag, 2008.

Helffer, Mireille; Macdonald, A. W., 'Sur un sarangi de Gâine', *Objets et Mondes*, 1966, V.6, 2, p. 133–142.

Helffer, Mireille; Macdonald, A. W., *Castes de musiciens au Népal*, Paris, Musée de l'Homme, 1969.

Hembron, Ruby (author); Jain, Boski (illustrator), *We come from the Geese*, Santal Creation Stories, New Delhi, Adivaani, 2013.

Hembron, Ruby (author); Jain, Boski (illustrator), *Earth rests on a Tortoise*, Santal Creation Stories, New Delhi, Adivaani, 2013.

Hembrom, Timotheus, *The Santals, Anthropological-Theological Reflections on Santaliand Biblical Creation Traditions*, Kolkata, Punthi Pustak, 1996.

Hembrom, Timotheas, *The Santal and the Biblical Creation Traditions. Anthropological & Theological Reflections*, Kolkata, Adivaani, 2013.

von der Heydt, Eduard, 'Ich sammle', *Inspire: Mode. Literatur. Kunst*, 1950, August, 2, 16, p. 7.

Illner, Eberhard (ed.), *Eduard von der Heydt: Kunstsammler, Bankier, Mäzen*, Munich, Prestel, 2013.

Ingold, Tim, *The Perception of the Environment: Essays on Livelihood, Dwelling and Skills*, New York, Routledge, 2000.

Janata, Alfred, *Musikinstrumente der Völker*, Vienna, Museum für Völkerkunde, 1975.

Kaiser, Thomas: *Bildrollen, Dauer und Wandel einer indischen Volkskunst*, Stuttgart, Arnoldsche Art Publishers, 2012. <http://www.arnoldsche.com/out/media/flippdf/365-4_Bildrollen_dt/>.

Kaiser, Thomas; Schütz, Samuel, *Klingende Bilder. Bildrollen wandernder Sänger in Bihar, Orissa und Bengalen*, Zurich, A.I.P./Büro 64, Museum Rietberg, 1999.

Kämpchen, Martin, *Das Geheimnis des Flötenspielers*, Wuppertal, Peter Hammer Verlag, 2000.

Kämpchen, Martin, 'Das Instrument der armen Leute', *Frankfurter Allgemeine Sonntagszeitung*, 2013, 10 November, no 45, p. 73.

Klein, Kathrin, *Die Santals – eine indische Stammesgesellschaft*, unpublished diploma thesis, 2006. Chapter 2.8 <http://www.dorfent-wicklung-indien.de/>.

Kothari, K. S., *Indian Folk Musical Instruments*, New Delhi, Sangeet Natak Akademi, 1968.

Menuhin, Yehudin, *La légende du violon*, Paris, Flammarion, 1996.

Michels, Ulrich (ed.), *dtv-Atlas zur Musik*, Munich, Bärenreiter Verlag, 1985.

Krishnaswami, S., *Musical Instruments of India*, New Delhi, Publications Division, Ministry of Information & Broadcasting, Government of India, 1965.

Miner, Allyn, *Sitar and Sarod in the 18th and 19th Centuries*, Wilhelmshaven, Florian Noetzel Verlag, 1993.

Mitter, Partha, *Indian Art*, Oxford, Oxford University Press, 2001.

Ong, Walter J. *Orality & Literacy: The Technologizing of the Word*, London, New York, New Accents Publication, Routledge, 1982.

Orans, Martin, *The Santal: a tribe in Search of a Great Tradition*, University of Chicago, Wayne State university Press, 1965.

Pannier, François, *Instruments de musique des Santal et des Ho*, Paris, Galerie Le Toit du Monde, 1991.

Pannier, François, *Santals. Dhodro Banam et panneaux palaquins*, unpublished manuscript of a conference at Musée du quai Branly, Paris, 1991.

Pesch, Ludwig, *Vom Klang des Glücks: ein Leitfaden zur Konzert-, Tanz- und Tempelmusik Südindiens*, Amsterdam, Eka.grata publications, 1996.

Pesch, Ludwig (ed.), *The Oxford Illustrated Companion to South Indian Classical Music*, New Delhi, Oxford University Press, 1999.

Platthaus, Andreas, 'So schön klingt die musikalische Migrantin', *Frankfurter Allgemeine Sonntagszeitung*, 10 November 2013, No. 45, p. 70.

Prasad, Onkar, *Santal Music. A Study in Pattern and Process of Cultural Persistence*, Tribal Studies of India Series, New Delhi, Inter-India Publications, 1985.

Prasad, Onkar, 'Text-Tune and Tone-Tune Relations in Santal Music: Some Preliminary Observations', Wade, Bonnie C. (ed.), *Text, Tone And Tune: Parameters of Music in Multicultural Perspective*, New Delhi, Oxford & IBH, 1993.

Ranade, Ashok D., 'Transmission of Nonclassical Traditions', *The Garland Encyclopedia of World Music, South Asia: The Indian Subcontinent*, New York, Garland Publishing, 1999, V. 5.

Rosenthal, Ethel, *The Story of Indian Music and its Instruments*, New Delhi, Munshiram Manoharlal Publishers Pvt. Ltd., 1980, (London, William Reeves, 1928).

Roy, Souvanic, *Santhal Architecture, Kolkata, Folk and Tribal Cultural Center*, Kolkata, 1998

Roy Chaudhury, Indu, 'Folk Tales of the Santals', *Folk Tales of India Series*, New Delhi, Sterling Publishers, 1973, V. 13.

Sachs, Curt, *Die Musikinstrumente Indiens und Indonesiens*, Berlin, W. De Gruyter, 1923 (1914).

Sadie, Stanley John (ed.), *The New Grove Dictionary of Musical Instruments*, London, Macmillan Press, 1984, 3 V.

Schneider, Marius, 'Musique, mythologies, rites', Roland-Manuel (ed.), *Histoire de la musique*, Encyclopédie de La Pléiade, Paris, Gallimard, 1960–1963, 2 V., 1961, V. 1, p. 131–214.

Sen, Sharmistha, *The String Instruments of North India*, New Delhi, 1988–1992, 2 V.

Shirali, Vishnudas, *An Introduction to Indian Music*, New Delhi, Abhinav/ Marg Publications, 1977.

Singh, Ajit K., *Tribal Festival of Bihar: A functional analysis*, New Delhi, Concept Publishing Company, 1982.

Stoller, Peter, Embodying *Colonial Memories: Spirit Possession, Power and the Hauka in West Africa*, New York, Routledge, 1995.

Tagore, Rabindranath, 'Meine Erinnerungen an Einstein', (1931), Kämpchen, Martin (ed.). *Das goldene Boot – Lyrik, Prosa, Dramen*, Düsseldorf, Zurich, Artemis & Winkler, 2005.

Tapati, Guha-Thakurta, 'The Period of Colonisalism and Nationalism, c. 1757–1947', Ascher, Frederic M. (ed.), *Art of India, Prehistory to the Present*, New Delhi, Encyclopedia Britanica, 2003, p. 109–128.

Taussig, Michael, *Mimesis and Alterity: A Particular History of the Senses*, New York, Routledge, 1993.

Tranchefort, François René, *Les instruments de musique dans le monde*, Paris, Seuil, 1980.

Troisi, J., *The Santals: A Classified and Annoted Bibliography*, New Delhi, Manohar Book Service, 1976.

Troisi, J., *Tribal Religion: Religious Beliefs and Practices among the Santals*, New Delhi, Manohar, 1978.

Vatsyayan, Kapila, *Traditions of Indian Folk Dance*, New Delhi, Indian Book Company, 1976. Vatsyayan, Kapila, Traditions of Indian Folk Dance, New Delhi, Clarion Books, 1976.

Viveiros de Castro, Eduardo, 'Exchanging Perspectives: The Transformation of Objects into Subjects in Amerindian Ontologies', *Common Knowledge*, 2004, 10, p. 463–484.

Waddell, Major Laurence Austine, *Among the Himalayas*, Westminster, Archibald Constable & Co., 1900, (1898). https://archive.org/stream/amonghimalayas00wadd

Yadav, Anumeha, 'Tribals torn apart by religion', The Hindu, 22 April 2014. <http://www.thehindu.com/opinion/op-ed/tribals-torn-apart-by-religion/article5934381.ece>.

ON-LINE RESOURCES

http://adivaani.org
http://www.bengtfosshag.de
http://www.daricha.org
http://www.indiantribalheritage.org
http://www.indiantribalheritage.org/?page_id=8352
http://www.indiantribalheritage.org/?p=15616
https://soundcloud.com/adivaani/
http://wesanthals.tripod.com/id1.html

AUDIO

Hansda, Gokul; Kämpchen, Martin (eds.), *Mein Liebling spielt die Flöte. Lieder des indischen Santal-Stammes*, Audio-CD, Boppard am Rhein/Salzburg, Boppard am Rhein, Fidula Verlag, 2008.

Bhattacharya, Deben, *Music of the Santal Tribe, Field recording by Deben Bhattacharya*, fields recordings made in 1954 and 1973, Audio-CD, Paris, ARC Music, 2014.

Battacharya, Deben, *Radio Talks, for the BBC and the Swedish Radio*, Original documents, Paris, Kolkata, Jhanrna Battacharya and Paris, National Library, 1954 and 1973.

Bosshard, Andres; Pannke, Peter, *Honey Wind. Sounds from a Santal Village (India)*, Audio-CD in Cooperation with IGNCA in November 1994, a Production of Sender Freies Berlin, Mainz, 1997.

VIDEO

*Banam. Myth and Cosmology of the Santhals*, IGNCA's intangible Heritage Series, Director: Bappa Ray, [1960], 42.57 min.

*Faces of the Forest*, a film on Santal by Beben Bhattacharya, 1973, 27 min.

*Banam Raja*, documentary by Joy Tudu, including the process of making an instrument and young Santals telling about their musical involvement between tradition and modernity, [2014], 13.22 min
.
http://www.indiantribalheritage.org/?page_id=15611

*Santal at the Crafts Museum, Chadar Badar-puppetry*, video by Sudhanshu Shandilya, 5 December 2014.

Front Cover: Photograph by Sudhanshu Shandilya, © Museum Rietberg, Zurich

Back Cover: Photograph by Alain Daniélou and Raymond Burnier (AD RB B 1135), © FIND, Zagarolo (Roma)

p. 7–17: Photographs by Alain Daniélou and Raymond Burnier (p. 7: AD RB B 1136; p. 8-9: RB C 79-2; p. 10: AD B 1145; p. 11: AD B 1137; p. 12-13: RB C 79-4; p. 14-15: RB C 140-13; p. 16: AD RB B 1135; p. 17: AD RB B 1134), © FIND, Zagarolo (Roma)

p. 29–41: Photographs by Deben Bhattacharya (p. 29: 12-73-020; p. 30: 12-73-031; p. 31 above: 13-73-001; p. 31 below: 12-73-013; p. 32: 12-73-001; p. 33: 12-73-024; p. 34: 12-73-025; p. 35 above: 12-73-011; p. 35 below: 12-73-008; p. 36: 13-73-023; p. 37: 14-73-001; p. 38: 14-73-002; p. 39: 14-73-013; p. 40: 13-73-003; p. 41 above: 13-73-005; p. 41 below: 13-73-026), Digitalisation by Brenda Turnnidge, © Jharna Bose Bhattacharya, Kolkata and Paris

p. 46: Photograph by Johannes Beltz, © Johannes Beltz, Zurich

p. 48–50: Photographs by Munshi Asif Iqbal, © Jayasri Banerjee, Kolkata and New Delhi

p. 55: Photograph by Sudhanshu Shandilya, © Museum Rietberg, Zurich

p. 58: Photograph by Ravi Kant Dwivedi, © Ravi Kant Dwivedi, New Delhi

p. 63–73: Photographs by Ravi Kant Dwivedi, © Ravi Kant Dwivedi, New Delhi

p. 77: Sketches by Ravi Kant Dwivedi, © Ravi Kant Dwivedi, New Delhi

p. 81, 83: Photographs by Ravi Kant Dwivedi, © Ravi Kant Dwivedi, New Delhi

p. 84–86: Photographs by Sudhanshu Shandilya, © Museum Rietberg, Zurich

p. 89–93: Photographs by Ravi Kant Dwivedi, © Ravi Kant Dwivedi, New Delhi

p. 95–99, 102–103: Photographs by Sudhanshu Shandilya, © Museum Rietberg, Zurich

p. 108–109: Photographs by Munshi Asif Iqbal, ©Jayasri Banerjee, Kolkata and New Delhi

p. 110 (1–3): © National Museum, New Delhi

p. 110–113: (4–18; 20–45): Photographs by Ingrid zur Buchen, © Museum Rietberg, Zurich

p. 111 (19): Photograph by Rainer Wolfsberger, © Museum Rietberg, Zurich

JAYASRI BANERJEE
is a professional sitar player and musicologist, with interest in both classical and popular traditions of music. Her early research was on teaching methodologies of classical music in institutional and non-institutional contexts. She has also worked on Adivasi music and musical instruments, and undertaken extensive fieldwork, documentation and advocacy of endangered musical genres.

JOHANNES BELTZ
holds a PhD in Religious Studies from the Universities of Paris and Lausanne. He worked for the South Asia Institute in Heidelberg from 1996 to 2004. In 2002 he joined the Museum Rietberg in Zurich, where he is curator of South and South East Asian art and heads the curatorial department. He teaches on Buddhism and Hinduism at the University of Zurich.

MARINE CARRIN
anthropologist, is Director of Research Emeritus (CNRS) at the Centre d'Anthropologie, Toulouse. Her books on Santals include *La Fleur et l'Os: Symbolisme et Rituel chez les Santal* (1986); *Enfants de la Déesse: Prêtrise et Devotion Féminine au Bengale* (1997); *Le Parler des Dieux* (in press) and *A Peripheral Encounter: Santals, Missionaries and their Changing Worlds* (with H. Tambs-Lyche, 2008).

MARIE-EVE CELIO-SCHEURER
holds a PhD in Art History from Paris IV-Sorbonne. She is a recipient of a grant from the Swiss National Science Foundation and was a Research Fellow at the German Institute for Art History in Paris. From 2004 to 2012, she lived in India where she worked as a consultant for UNESCO (India) on museum issues. She is currently scientific collaborator at the Museum Rietberg.

RAVI KANT DWIVEDI
graduated in Fine Arts from Kala Bhawan, Santiniketan. He is a photographer and a documentary filmmaker. For more than 35 years he has been involved in research and documentation of folk and tribal arts and culture. He has travelled extensively in remote area and mostly on foot. Chadar Badar, Santal puppetry, was first researched and documented by him.

RUCHIRA GHOSE
took her Tripos and PhD in Economics from Cambridge University, U.K. Since 1994 she has been working in the field of Craft and Design. In 2010 she was appointed Chairman of the Crafts Museum, New Delhi, where she has initiated a major programme of renewal and revitalization.

BENGT FOSSHAG
worked as graphic designer for international companies. As illustrator and cartoonist he contributed regularly to renowned magazines and newspapers. He is well known as a collector of Indian and African tribal art. In 2012 he offered his outstanding collection of Indian stringed instruments to the Museum Rietberg.

MUSHTAK KHAN
graduated in Fine Arts and Inorganic Chemistry from Jiwaji University, Gwalior. He has researched and documented the craft sector for more than 30 years. He was Deputy Director at the Crafts Museum, New Delhi for 24 years and has continued as Research Consultant to contribute to the work of the Museum.

MALLIKA LEUZINGER
holds a BA in History and MPhil in Gender Studies from Cambridge University, U.K. She grew up in Bangalore and currently works at the Fotomuseum Winterthur in Switzerland.

ALBERT LUTZ
holds a PhD in East Asian Art History with a special focus on Chinese art from Zurich University. In 1982 he joined the Museum Rietberg, where he has been the Director since 1998. He enlarged the museum with a new extension in 2007 and has curated numerous exhibitions with cross-cultural themes.

KRITTIKA NARULA
holds a Masters in Art History from the National Museum Institute, New Delhi. She has worked on several research and curatorial projects on South Asian decorative arts and textiles. Since 2014, she has been working as Research Consultant at the Crafts Museum, New Delhi.

LUDWIG PESCH
is a musician and musicologist trained in Freiburg University, Germany, and Kalakshetra, India. His special interest is in mutual learning beyond conventional disciplines. He wrote *The Oxford Illustrated Companion to South Indian Classical Music* and was awarded the Cross of the Order of Merit by the President of the Federal Republic of Germany for his contribution to cultural relations with India.

# ACKNOWLEDGEMENTS

This has been a richly collaborative project, involving many institutions and individuals in several countries. We have been uniquely privileged to have the support of so many who have contributed with such grace and goodwill to the final outcome. The starting point of the project has of course been the amazing musical stringed instruments of the Bengt Fosshag collection. We convey our heartfelt gratitude to the collector.

The project would not have been possible without the generous financial support of the Swiss Federal Office of Culture (FOC). Our special thanks go to Benno Widmer, Head of the Specialized Body for International Transfer of Cultural Property at the Swiss Federal office of Culture and Marco Eichenberger, scientific collaborator.

This book would not have been possible without the important contribution from Accentus Foundation, Elena Probst Fonds. It is a privilege to receive the generous support of partners engaged in inter-museum cooperation.

UNESCO has played a decisive role in the project, which commenced with the engagement of a consultant to promote partnership between Museums in India and in Europe, focussing on preservation of cultural heritage and long-term capacity building. We would like to express our gratitude especially to Shigeru Aoyagi, Director and UNESCO representative to Bhutan, Maldives, India and Sri Lanka, and Moe Chiba, Programme Specialist for Culture. Our thanks as well to Vijay Raghavan, Programme Assistant for Culture, for organising a workshop on Intangible Heritage.

The Embassy of Switzerland in India has played a most supportive role. We are extremely grateful to Ambassador Dr. Linus von Castelmur and his wife, Françoise Gardies who have helped to ensure the fruition of the project. Our warm thanks go as well to Sarah Bernasconi, First Secretary and Cultural Officer, who facilitated the project at every stage.

We would like to extend our warmest thanks to all those involved at the National Museum in hosting and organising the exhibition, especially Dr. Venu Vasudevan, Director General, as well as to Joyoti Roy, Outreach Head; Anju Sachdeva, Deputy Curator, Anthropology; RK Verma, Deputy Curator, Exhibitions; Sushmit Sharma, Technical Assistant. Our warmest thanks also to Indira Gandhi Rashtriya Manav Sangrahalaya, Bhopal, especially Professor Sarit Kumar Chaudhuri, Director, for his support and collaboration.

The core team of the project includes, first and foremost, Mushtak Khan, Senior Consultant at the Crafts Museum whose profound knowledge of craft and of tribal traditions has made him an essential and invaluable resource. Ravi Kant Dwivedi, Krittika Narula and Mallika Leuzinger assisted ably and amply in the research. Krittika Narula, in addition, played an important role in organising the various materials for book and exhibition and was assisted by Shibani Das, Project Intern. Each worked in a sincere and pertinent way, and very comfortably together, to assure the quality of the project. We express our special gratitude also to Jayasri Banerjee, Marine Carrin and Ludwig Pesch, all of whom shared their original research and documentation.

For sources and documentation, we would like also to thank the Bibliothèque Nationale in Paris, especially Pascal Cordereix for his dedication, as well as India-Europe Foundation for New Dialogues (FIND) in Zagarolo (Roma), which houses photographic archives of Alain Daniélou and Raymond Burnier on the Santal community. Our gratitude goes too to Jacques Cloarec, President of FIND, for his hospitality and support. Our warmest appreciation and thanks also go to Jharna Bhattacharya Bose, wife of the musicologist, the late Deben Bhattacharya, who shared her archives in Paris and Kolkata. Our sincere gratitude and thanks go to Ruby Hembrom and her team at Adivaani in Kolkata. Ruby has shared her knowledge and resources most generously, which have added quality and depth to the exhibition.

In the complex and painstaking task of producing the book, the contribution of Malini Saigal as Editor and the graphic designers Pierre Girardin and Philippe Karrer of ECAL Lausanne, have been invaluable. We are most grateful to them and to Alexis Gorgacopulos, Director of ECAL, who agreed to support the venture.

We extend our warmest thanks to the photographers Sudhanshu Shandilya, in New Delhi, who worked at the Crafts Museum while the Santal artists were in residence in December 2014, Brenda Turnnidge, in Paris, who worked on the photographic archives of Deben Bhattacharya, Rainer Wolfsberger, in Zurich and Ingrid zur Buchen, in Hattersheim am Main, who photographed the Bengt Fosshag collection.

We would like to thank Jacqueline Schöb and Martin Sollberger, respectively the graphic designer and the scenographer at the Museum Rietberg, Zurich, and Kanu Kartik Agrawal, scenographer for the exhibition at the National Museum, New Delhi, for their help and direction.

Many individuals supported us with information and with documentation. We would like to thank especially Laurent Aubert, France Grand, Cornelia Mallebrein, François Pannier, Jean-Claude Plattner. Our gratitude goes to Bikash and Tultul Niyogi, who assure the quality and the distribution of this publication.

Finally, we extend our warmest thanks and appreciation to the Santal craftsmen with whom we had the privilege to interact: Babudhan Murmu, Bhulu Murmu, Shibdhan Murmu, Sonadhan Murmu, as well as Sangeeta Murmu and Yashodi Murmu.

Johannes Beltz, Marie-Eve Celio-Scheurer, Ruchira Ghose

# IMPRESSUM

The present publication accompanies the exhibition 'Sculpted Sound: Stringed Instruments from India' at the Museum Rietberg, Zurich, 4 September 2014–19 April 2015 and the exhibition 'Cadence and Counterpoint: Documenting Santal Musical Traditions' co-curated by the Museum Rietberg and the Crafts Museum, New Delhi and exhibited at the National Museum, New Delhi, 15 April–17 May 2015.

Chief editors: Johannes Beltz and
Marie-Eve Celio-Scheurer, Museum Rietberg, Zurich, and
Ruchira Ghose, Crafts Museum, New Delhi

Project initiation and coordination:
Marie-Eve Celio-Scheurer and Ruchira Ghose

Adviser: Mushtak Khan, Crafts Museum, New Delhi

Research assistant: Krittika Narula, Crafts Museum, New Delhi

Translation: (from German to English) Mallika Leuzinger, Zurich, Simon Pickstone, London; (from Santali to English) Ravi Kant Dwivedi, New Delhi

Photography: Sudhanshu Shandilya, New Delhi, Brenda Turnnidge, Paris, Rainer Wolsfberger, Zurich, Ingrid zur Buchen, Hattersheim a. M.

Published by
NIYOGI BOOKS
D-78, Okhla Industrial Area, Phase-I
New Delhi-110 020, INDIA
Tel: 91-11-26816301, 49327000
Fax: 91-11-26810483, 26813830
email: niyogibooks@gmail.com
website: www.niyogibooksindia.com



Editor: Malini Saigal
Graphic Concept and Book design:
Pierre Girardin, Philippe Karrer, Lausanne
Typeface: RH Inter by Robert Hubert, Lausanne

ISBN: 978-93-83098-92-7
Publication: 2015



Printed at: Niyogi Offset Pvt. Ltd., New Delhi, India

शिल्प संग्रहालय
Crafts Museum

NATIONAL MUSEUM - New Delhi

museum rietberg

Schweizerische Eidgenossenschaft
Confédération suisse
Confederazione Svizzera
Confederaziun svizra

Swiss Confederation

Federal Department of Home Affairs FDHA
**Federal Office of Culture FOC**

Schweizerische Eidgenossenschaft
Confédération suisse
Confederazione Svizzera
Confederaziun svizra

**Embassy of Switzerland in India**

United Nations
Educational, Scientific and
Cultural Organization

**New Delhi Office**
Cluster Office for Bangladesh, Bhutan, India, Maldives, Nepal and Sri Lanka

écal

ACCENTUS